KEMBALI ~ RETURN
OF THE MYSTIC

JAN TAKI

Dr. JAN
2012

Published by **Pouldrew Press**,
Portlaw, Co. Waterford, Ireland.

Email: **pouldrewpress@gmail.com**

© Pouldrew Press, Second Edition - December 2011

ISBN: 978-0-9570525-0-5

Printed by Imprint Digital, Exeter in the UK,
on paper from sustainable forests.

Proofing, typesetting & cover design: **eimear@wordworks.net**

From the Author

This book is a semi-autobiography, written with a huge dollop of fantasy and a large pinch of mischief. Do not do as I do, for it will get you nowhere. Just do as I say, as all good doctors will tell you. And this is no ordinary doctor.

Many of the characters were real when they existed in their time and some new ones came a-calling in the middle of my sleepless nights, begging inclusion into my story.

Who am I to refuse? Read on!

The author wishes to thank all his friends and patients for their help and encouragement in the writing of this book.

Special thanks to Walther Graf von Krenner, Teresa Murphy, Dato Lim Kee Jin and Datin Pat, Dr. Shan, Larry Senior, Edward Power, Gavin Maxwell, Eimear Gallagher, Karen T. Colbert, and Billy O'Dwyer Bob.

This book is dedicated to the memory of my Masters and friends...... Fat Aunt, Pak Samad, Aweh, Badang, and Sri, for a life lived in vivid colour.

Written for ......
Phoenix and Julian Bosshardt
Vienna and Jim Strader
With Love ......

Glossary

Here is an explanation of the terms and an introduction to the main characters you will meet in *Kembali ~ Return Of The Mystic.*

Ah Jan (later known as Si Jan and Jepun): the main character is a boy reborn to a family in Singapore, just after the Second World War. Ah Jan has a memory of a former life as an Officer in the Imperial Japanese Army. He sets about trying to trace his Past Life, and, in the process, meets a bunch of Mystics who guide him in that direction, while transforming him into a Mystic as well. 'Si' (as in 'Si Jan') is a title given to any man worthy of respect, usually a mature male, while 'Ah' (as in 'Ah Jan') is a term of endearment.

Aweh: one of Si Jan's Mystic Masters, his friend and companion, who can still kill on the human plane. He shows Si Jan how the future can be accessed and even changed.

Badang: another of Si Jan's Mystic Masters, Badang teaches Si Jan the art of remote healing, not only of people, but everything —be it plant, rock, animal or human.

Fat Aunt: Si Jan's cook who becomes his first Master and teaches him the Secrets of the Mau San or Chinese Shamanism, which results in his first near-fatal attempt at Invisibility.

Datok: ancient Chief and Governor of that part of Hari Kong.

Grey Winds: These are the Magic Winds that criss-cross the world, providing Mystics, be they Good or Bad, with a convenient way to travel.

Hari Kong: This is the extra day in a week for Mystics, also known as the 'Eighth Day'. Invisible to the uninitiated, it is a place in between mortal time; Mystics can retreat into Hari Kong to become invisible, to find space to heal themselves, to travel unnoticed or do battle amongst themselves.

Kanemoto: This is the name of the Japanese sword that Kyai Aweng changes into when ordered. It bears the name of its maker, Kanemoto, a famous swordsmith in old Japan.

Kembali: means 'return' in Malay.

Kriyat: name of an invisible spear, given by Pak Samad to Si Jan that only appears when summoned; it always does Si Jan's bidding.

Kyai Aweng: name of the magic keris that Aweh makes for Si

Jan. Forged with his bare hands when the metal was still red hot, it has the power to transform itself into any other weapon Si Jan needs in his battles with the Evil Forces.

Mat Hijau and Rahim: the two 'were tigers' that help Si Jan become invulnerable after capturing the Spirit of Cane.

Nosey, Johnny, Ramasamy, Ah Chee And Mong Hiang: childhood friends of Si Jan.

Pak Samad: the legendary warrior Hang Tuah, he was also the Laksamana or Admiral during the Malaccan Sultanate in the 15th Century. He is now in disguise to lure Si Jan deeper into the Realms of Mysticism.

Princess of Gunong Ledang: Known in Malaysian Legends as the Ruler of the sacred mountain, Mt. Ophir, she is rumoured to have married Hang Tuah.

Spirit of Cane: a magical piece of petrified wood, ritually extracted from a rattan jungle cane and inserted under the skin of the recipient, the 'Spirit of Cane' makes the subject invulnerable to metal.

Sri Pelangi or "Sri": a pretty lady-in-waiting to the Princess who agrees to marry Ah Jan.

See also pages 213 and 214 for background information on the weapons that form part of this story.

Chapter One

You may call me Ah Jan. I was born not long after the Second World War, in the month of October, Year of the Fire Pig, and at the hour of the Tiger.

When I was born, I was conscious of human speech, understanding all the three languages spoken around me while I lay swathed in a light-coloured woolen blanket.

I was also conscious that I had lived before as a Japanese Officer who was killed by a group of Burmese villagers when my two men and I took refuge in their village after our retreat from Kohima, a town not far from the Burmese-Indian border.

I was killed with my own sword while we slept in sheer exhaustion at the base of a wooden tower.

My last memory of that life was a vision of a group of laughing Burmese villagers as they surrounded us to watch our death throes. I felt no pain, only sadness to see my life end under such circumstances and without a fight.

I remember taking leave of my mortal coil and floating above my two blood-soaked comrades. I remember barking an order for them to rise, but they laid still and unmoving under that mud-stained, wooden structure.

I have no idea how long my soul or spirit spent like a trapped fly, bouncing from one wall to the next of this black box. There were times when I could glimpse through chinks of light to show me what was happening on the battlefield below. There were other times when I could see our Army's defeat and then our hurried retreat from the Burmese mountains and down the plains towards Rangoon. All the while I was just a helpless and frustrated observer, barking orders and advice to my men below, orders that no one could hear.

I did try, in spirit, to return home to my own country Japan, but each time I could only see as far as the dark sea and the sight of the same troop ship reflected in the moonlight below. Somehow, my sight and memory became limited and I felt chained to this part of a limbo. I must have stayed there for a while, bathed in anger and hatred, unable to accept the fact that I was dead, and still wanting to carry on the fight for our Emperor.

Sometime later, the blackness around me lifted and I became conscious of being transformed into a small twig floating on a cold jungle stream ready to be washed down into another incarnation.

You can say that I was flushed down the stream of life into one probably not of my own choosing. Maybe it was a throw of dice by some hand called Destiny. I know not, all I know is that I was reborn to a family in Singapore or Syonan-to [Light of the South], the name we gave that island when we conquered her in 1942.

I realised very soon that I had been born into a house of wealth when it was plain to see that servants in the house outnumbered the members of the family.

I was their first born, their only son. I only smiled each time they cuddled me and tried to engage me in "baby talk". I would normally close my eyes and feign sleep.

My grandfather passed away when I was only nine months old. But I can still remember the time he held me in his arms a few months before his demise. And what was spoken in Malay by a boy on the beach looking for his ball when he spotted women folk crying, as they watched the boat sail out with grandfather's cremated ashes, to be scattered in the sea. "Oi!! Keep quiet, there are women crying here," he shouted to his friends in Malay.

All the while, I was an adult in a baby's body, but only as an observer. I felt no sorrow at the event, because I never felt that I was Ah Jan. *I am someone else. What name, what rank and which unit of the Imperial Japanese Army?* That, I could never recall.

There were times, even as a baby, when I tried hard to remember my past life, and was even able to utter a few Japanese words out of the blue, much to the surprise and astonishment of my family who could speak in English, Chinese and Malay but not in Japanese.

They often considered me unusual, if not weird, to be so precocious. Friends of my father predicted that I would be a genius one day, some said that I had been "here before" or that I "came from Above".

I suppose that this was all to please my father, if not to allay his fears that his son might be a freak.

As a child, I always preferred adult company. At the age of four or so, I was able to understand, reason and even contribute to their discussions. But I always held my tongue, whenever the atrocities of the Japanese Army were being discussed. Something kept me from betraying my "hidden self". I harboured a secret, a dark secret.

I just listened, nodded and took in their accounts as though I were there when all that happened, not so long ago.

The bayoneting, the beheadings sounded familiar to my young ears. I had no nightmares and sleep was always a welcome rest from the torment of a soul seeking recognition, escape or release.

The tunnels that the Japanese Army built under the Bukit Panjang hills fascinated me, and I always asked to be brought there. My servants tried their best to frighten me out of this obsession. Ghosts, snakes and bombs were often enlisted in their gruesome tales about those tunnels. I wasn't frightened in the least.

One day, when I was about nine, I gave them the slip and went in as far as the daylight allowed me. I never knew I needed a torch or where to find one. I was given a sound thrashing when they found me and realised where I had gone and what I had done. There is more than one use for a feather duster, I soon discovered.

After all, I was their precious son, and heir to the family name.

When I was eleven, I found a new friend called Mong Hiang. He was the son of a market gardener and lived in the depth of the then Singapore countryside. There were rubber estates and farms hidden between the foothills of Bukit Panjang [Long Range Hill] and the sea to the west of the island.

That was the place where the Main Force of Gen. Tomoyuki Yamashita landed from across the Johor Straits to conquer Singapore in 1942.

It was to become my playground. Many a day after school would find me in his farm where the Japanese trenches were located, trenches dug and used by the first wave of landed troops and then abandoned as they leap-frogged from one trench to the next heading south, towards the city, leaving their unused mortar shells and other ammunition for those coming up from behind.

Memories came flooding back, each time I sat in one of those trenches. I used to look up to see if I could still spot a fleeing Australian digger or two, so that I could shout a command to shoot and kill. *"Utemi! UTEMI!"*

I could almost hear my old voice and vaguely picture my old self leading the assault. There were times when I was near to the point of remembering who I was before. But each time, the setting of the sun signalled my return to the present moment and I knew that I must hurry home as I would be missed at dinner time and another tryst with the feather duster would be a dead certainty.

And so I lived my younger years, with one mind in my past and one as a child relearning what I already knew, though in a different language, in a different school and a different land.

Every morning at sunrise, when we had our school assembly and stood in neat rows facing the Headmaster, no one saw me make that slight bow, not to him but to our Amaterasu, the Sun Goddess and to our Emperor Hirohito. The word *"Banzai!"* was always close at the tip of my tongue and my hands, which should have been raised in salutation, were held down with clenched fists so as not to betray my old identity.

It was a hard task for a boy to do every morning, from the age of seven.

I found my first Arisaka bayonet in one of the trenches, together with a few horse shoes, under a layer of red bricks amongst the dead leaves of a rubber tree. I managed to sneak them home and hide my treasures under the dining room table.

Draped by a heavy cloth of Eastern brocade, that deep cavern so created was to become home to many of my excavated treasures from the trenches. Amongst them were two unexploded Japanese 88mm mortar shells.

The Gods were much kinder then, and allowed me time to grow up to realise that a meal might suddenly blow up in one's face, and no blame could be attached to Ah Fei Sum [Fat Aunt], our cook.

Chapter Two

F at Aunt did not take too long to get used to me. She came to our family to work as a cook when I was about three. She was quiet on her first few days at the job, learning the ropes, I suppose, or where the pots and pans should be. But after less than a week, she accepted me as a genius or freak who could speak Cantonese much better than she could and with far more ideas and points of view than anyone breathing.

For the first few weeks, she was moody with whatever past she dragged in with her when she came. She sulked, but I was eager to make friends and listen to this newcomer's story, and I persevered. So, many a night, I sat in the servants' room, together with the other two ladies, Lei Wah and Ah Mui, when the others were asleep and presumed me to be.

Fat Aunt was sold by her elder sister to a travelling troupe of Chinese opera performers, not long after her father died, when she was fourteen. Illiterate and apparently useless as a singer, she was let go not long after. She found work as a waitress in a tea shop that catered for labourers and the like. Life was tough, the hours rough, and the clients rougher. But she accepted her lot and hoped for better days to come.

Well, days came but not better ones. She found love in the arms of a gold miner and followed him to the Australian-run Gold Mine in Pahang. They had a daughter, but then, not long after, Ah Sam, the husband, was killed in a mining disaster.

When we, the Japanese Army, invaded Malaya, she was unable to support herself and the daughter. The daughter was given away to some strangers and, being illiterate, Fat Aunt had no idea to whom or to where she was taken. She drifted along and found work wherever she could until Fate took her to our door. So much she told her fellow-amahs or housemaids.

But she told me more in the following years. I became very attached to her. Her nickname Fei Sum or Fat Aunt was all I knew her as. She never told me her real name and I never asked. What if she turned around and asked me mine? It certainly was not Ah Jan. Maybe a Yamamoto or a Hashimoto. But, Ah Jan, never! I let it be. She called me by what the rest of the family called me, 'Ah Chai' [the Son].

Over the years, Fat Aunt and I shared a few secrets, little ones.

She was addicted to gambling on the 'Twelve sticks', the Chap Ji Ki, a popular pastime with all Chinese servants the country over. It is a two-digit lottery of twelve numbers, announced each day by the bookie. One day the result might be a two and a seven; perhaps a six and a five the next.

A written clue was always given by the syndicate the day before as to what the following day's numbers might be. So if the slip of paper, brought in by the ticket collector, said 'Old scholar on mule riding East', the next day's lottery result might be a four and an eight. You might win a few dollars with your bet of fifty cents.

Fat Aunt used to get Lay Wah to read the clues on the slip and the three ladies would make their guesses and bet on the next day's outcome.

"Seven Six," said one. "No! It's going to be a Two Four," predicted the other.

I was normally asked to make the last call. "It's a Three Seven," I would declare. I proved to be right on many an occasion, and there was often a packet of coconut candy waiting for me on those happy occasions. One day, I got tired of those sweets when my prediction proved true. All three ladies bought me a packet of coconut candy, I was ready to be sick. So I took Fat Aunt aside, and asked her if she would be kind enough to make me some Manju cakes.

"Wha! What do you know about Manju cakes?" she said. "Manju cakes are only eaten by the bloody Japanese you know!"

"Yes, I liked them when Grandma made them for me," I lied. And so, we had a deal. I got Manju Cakes and even charcoal-braised eel with soya sauce and sugar, Japanese style, if I made the correct predictions. She grew fatter with our secret feasts of Manju Cakes, and merrier as the few dollars flowed in.

One day, when I was seven or eight years old, Fat Aunt asked me if I had ever tasted rice wine.

"I have," I said, confidently.

"Where?"

"In Ah Soh's place, when her Grandfather died and they laid out three bowls for the Gods at the altar."

"You mean you stole the wine meant for the Gods? Or the dead?"

"Well, there were no Gods or Devils that I could see and the family were outside the house, crying and burning joss sticks and whatever," I said. "I drank all three bowls and ran back here and hid under the blanket in bed."

She laughed her head off.

"So that explains why there was such commotion then, at their house. Ha-ha-ha. There was talk that the Gods were so powerful that they came down from Heaven and drank all three bowls of wine!" Fat Aunt was beside herself with laughter. "They are even planning to build a shrine for Guan Kong, the Red-Faced General, the God of War. They think it must have been him, as he is known to have loved wine when he was on this Earth."

"Let them," I said.

So we planned our next project in secret—the making of our glutinous rice wine! I knew where Grandma kept the big cheng or wine-brewing urn. Fat Aunt lifted it from the storeroom without much effort.

With her substantial earnings from her Chap Ji Ki or the Twelve Sticks lottery, we bought three catties or six pounds of rice and yeast. We were dead quiet in the storeroom, as we spooned out the layers of cooked rice and yeast and the sprinkling of sugar, layer by layer, until the jar was almost full. We were each to our own thoughts as we placed the cover back on and wrapped the urn with thick sheets of newspaper, then hid the urn and closed the door. Being the cook, only she had the key.

Many weeks passed during which we shared our little secret with smiles every time we passed the storeroom door. Then one day she decided that the time was ripe to inspect our work since the others were away and the coast was clear. As we opened the jar, the fragrance of the still-fermenting mash wafted up. We helped ourselves to a bowl each of the reddish mash. It was sweet, and a bit heady.

"You know, I was also a Mau San," she confided after her third bowl, her face turning redder with the mash.

"You, a Mau San?" I asked.

"A Chinese Mystic? A Magician?"

"Yes. When I was stranded in Mentakab in Pahang, I followed a Mau San Sifu or Master to survive, and learned a lot of his magic."

"Like what?"

"Well, a Mau San can cast spells, fly through the air, become invisible, and drive away demons."

"Do you want to see me disappear?" she asked.

"Yes, yes, show me!" I said, while finishing my second bowl of mash.

"First I need three joss sticks, three nails, and three bunches of spring onions," she said.

"They are all in the kitchen," I volunteered.

"Okay, fetch them " she ordered while on her fourth bowl.

When the joss sticks were lit, she placed the three nails and the three bunches of spring onions on the table, stood at this makeshift altar of ours, and bowed low. I was then made to stand in front of her and closer to her "altar".

"We Mau Sans can disappear after three claps with our hands," she said, her face getting even redder. She stood behind me, and I heard her clap. Once, twice, thrice. And then silence.

I turned around and she was gone! I became a child of eight again. I yelled for her to come back. Well, all the other servants and my Grandma came back from their shopping expedition all right, but there was no sign of Fat Aunt. Her half-finished fifth bowl of mash was still on the table, and so were her meagre belongings on her bed. Missing was her mirror and comb and the well-worn and yellowing photograph of her husband and daughter taken before the War.

No one dared touch the mash, the jar washed clean and replaced in the storeroom. Nothing much was said by anyone that day, and no one believed my story.

Chapter Three

F at Aunt returned the next day carrying a hissing goose in a wicker basket in one arm and a bunch of kangkong [morning glory leaves] in the other.

"Where have you been?" the household shouted. I was of course glad to see her again, so were the two servants, but not my grandmother.

"Thank your gods that Master and Missus are away till next week, or you would have lost your job," Gran admonished.

"Well, I had an inkling as to where my elder sister might be," Fat Aunt replied, "so I took the first bus into the city."

"So, did you find her?"

"No, but certain parts of the city looked familiar," she said. "Maybe the next time I will be lucky."

Well, there was no talk about the mash and the claims I made about her being a Mau San. I was branded a dirty liar and a probable alcoholic when I grew up.

"No more making of rice wine OK?" Gran commanded.

This was good enough for me. Japanese Sake is never so sweet. It should be drunk from little cups poured from a Sake Zuki, the liquid warmed to the temperature between a lady's thighs.

Well, all these details, the Chinese civilians know little of, nor would I enlighten them. Ever since Fat Aunt's disappearance and my account of her being a Mau San, no one took me seriously.

"But how can Fat Aunt disappear so suddenly after clapping her hands thrice?" I once protested.

"With two bowls of fermenting mash in you, anything can disappear," said Lay Wah, the old faithful servant. "So, no more talk about your Japanese Army and being here before. Your mother did have a lot of rice wine just before you were born, so that accounts for your weird imaginings."

I smiled.

When things settled somewhat in the household and I was left alone again with Fat Aunt, I asked her why she had not backed me up in my story about her disappearance.

"Hush! Such things are not for discussing. That was our secret, remember?"

"Can I see you do it again? Will you teach me that, one day?"

"Yes, when you are older and can see some sense," she replied.

See sense? If only she knew. I was years older than she was. When my unit crashed through the Malay jungles and conquered the land, she would only have been a teenage bride married to that gold miner in Pahang. But such things are not for the discussing, as she so rightly said.

I started to feel quite wary of her—this jolly woman who could suddenly disappear after clapping her hands. I knew it had nothing to do with the mash I'd devoured. And I was not one to tell lies. Only little white ones. Sometimes.

So years passed by and I became more involved with my present life, as a schoolboy in Singapore. My former life as a Japanese officer gradually became less important as the day-to-day routine at school, and my friends there, replaced the memories of dead comrades stranded in some far-off jungle all those years ago.

I had to keep up my position in class as their top student, class monitor and later as the school's head prefect. There was little time for day-dreaming and probably wishful thinking as to who might be left of my family in post-war Japan. And I wondered if I had been married before.

One day, as Fat Aunt passed me at the kitchen table, I asked her, more out of curiosity than desire, "Eh Ah Fat Aunt, can anyone be a Mau San?" It had been years since her magical act of disappearing the Mau San way.

She laughed. "Only if you have that Mystic streak in you. Why? Do you want to be a Mau San too?"

"Yes! I'd like very much to be like you!"

"A Mau San's life is a tough one," she said. "Fate will throw all kinds of tragedies at you, to toughen you up so that you can be strong enough to help the weak when they come to you."

"I'm not afraid of anything," I replied, while folding away my books on the table. "What kind of tragedies?"

"Tragedy in love, money, and life," she said, looking more seriously at me. "And you may even die in the process. You are their only son, so be good, study hard and be a great man, like your father."

I became silent when I realised the responsibility that I owed to this set of parents of mine, and I told myself that I was their only son and they had high hopes for me.

"Fat Aunt," I said, "can I see you do some more Mau San magic? I promise I will not tell a soul."

"Soon enough, soon enough," she said as she scrubbed the wok and started to prepare the evening meal.

Weeks passed, it was at the time of the Mooncake Festival,

the fifteenth day of the eighth month, a day of the full moon to mark the day when the cruel Mongols of Kublai Khan were overthrown in long-ago China. The anniversary of that day is celebrated by Chinese the world over with mooncakes, a kind of Chinese pastry stuffed with sweet lotus seed fillings with a salted egg yolk in the centre to represent the full moon. And the children carry lighted paper lanterns made in the form of a fish, chicken or dragon, each suspended by a string hanging from a stick of bamboo. They take great delight, going as a group to illuminate the darker lanes of the village, munching on mooncakes as they go.

As a teenager by then, I could only sit by the balcony, eating slices of mooncake and watching them go about their perambulations. The moon became obscured not long after and the children's voices grew fainter as they walked further down the lane. The garden became a dark place, and I was at the point to going back to the house when, suddenly, from the corner of my eye, I spotted a lighted lantern moving across the garden, some ten yards from me, towards the clump of banana trees. Maybe it was the now-obscured moon, for it was impossible for me to see who was carrying the light. The lantern swayed as it moved on, silently, deeper into the patch of banana trees. There it stayed, unmoving as if waiting for my response.

"Who is it?" I called out. There was no reply, the lantern swayed yet again, waiting for further action from my side. I clambered over the railings of the balcony and walked towards the light. *What is a light to an Officer of the Imperial Japanese Army?* The lantern moved a bit closer into the depth of the grove.

"Fat Aunt! You scared me!" I cried, now as a startled teenager.

"How can you be a Mau San, if you are afraid of ghosts and demons?" she laughed.

"How did you walk by without my spotting you? I only saw the lantern! I thought it was a ghost," I said.

"Ha ha, you want to learn the Mau San way, don't you?" she chuckled. "Come, meet my Master, my Mau San Sifu."

"Where is your Sifu or Master?"

"Here!" she said, pointing to an empty patch of ground, now only lit by the light of her lantern. All I could see were three shiny spikes of metal, probably brass, pegged on the ground, and red string linking them to make a triangle.

"Where is he?" I asked, now getting more worried as the minutes ticked by. Fat Aunt started mumbling a prayer and made me hold the lantern. Using her fingers, she made strange signs, tying them in a knot, then untying them to form another. I was mesmerised just watching her fingers making strange forms such as I'd never seen anyone make before.

She stopped, looked at me, smiled and in the flickering light of the lantern nodded her head towards the space in the clearing.

I nearly dropped the lantern. There sat an old man. His white hair was tied up in a knot by a piece of red cloth and his beard, also white, flowed down his chest. He wore the robes of a wandering mendicant, a penniless medicine man, a Mystic or a Mau San. He sat motionless as Fat Aunt knelt and bade me do the same.

"Sifu, this young boy here wants to join our Order," she said in her softest voice. "What is your opinion?" Still bowing, she nudged me and asked me to be quick. "Say you want to be a Mau San! Be quick!"

I looked up at the old man, and in the still flickering light I could see the piercing glare of his ancient eyes. As he looked at me, he smiled and said: "This man hasn't really left his past life. He still has to find completion before he can really start living this present one. Your wife Kumiko is still alive." He then looked away, ignoring me.

Fat Aunt gazed at me in total surprise. "So all the talk about you being a former Japanese Officer—is it true?" Before I could nod an answer, there was a sound like a clap of thunder. We looked up and her Sifu was nowhere to be seen. Kumiko? Kumiko? I kept repeating the name as we walked back to the house. The candle in the lantern had long burned out.

For days, Fat Aunt ignored me. I was her dreaded Japanese soldier, one of those who made her suffer so much during the war. She had to give up her daughter, all because of me!

What could I say? I was only a lad of fourteen.

Chapter Four

My school days spent in the Raffles Institution were done on auto pilot. I was neither here with this world or the one where I had lived and died before. I made more trips to Mong Hiang's vegetable farm and dug up more relics of the last war to recover more memories. I even found a helmet with some hair of the last wearer inside. No sign of the skull, the tin hat was of Australian manufacture, so it must have belonged to a Teki or enemy. I was happy to see the bullet hole on its side.

There were many boxes of unused ammunition meant for our Arisaka 98 rifles and more horse shoes under a rotting canvas sheet. I could feel our dead hovering around together with the large colony of mosquitoes. I often wondered if we reincarnate as such pests. Buzzing around my ears, I could almost hear them sing me some song in Japanese. What were they trying to tell me? To give up looking for myself, or to carry on?

The name 'Kumiko' meant nothing to me at all. I could not put a face on it. Hard for a boy of sixteen to visualise a wife, waiting in Japan. I was neither here or there, so I just drifted with the tide and, as they say, I just 'played along' with what this present Life threw at me. I hardly paid attention at school or studied when I reached home. I dreamt one day into the next.

One Saturday morning, as I came away from our National Museum on Stamford Road, I noticed a group of Japanese tourists outside a row of shops that sold handbags of crocodile skin.

Like so many Japanese tourists, they were dressed in summer wear, sporting sunglasses and tropical sun hats. As I neared them, I whispered: *"Kumiko san!"*

The group froze, turned in my direction, and a lady amongst them answered.

"Hai!" she said. I was speechless as I gazed at her. She was middle-aged, plump, had badly-formed teeth and wore a pair of oversized sunglasses.

"Sumi masen, shikashi watakushi wa O-shi Shoko deshita. Buramu no senso tsutomeru shimashita."

"Excuse me, I am Japanese," I said, then blurted out, "I was a Japanese Officer in Burma during the last Asiatic War."

"Aso desu ka?" said the man beside her as he placed a

protective arm around his Kumiko. The group looked at me, this sixteen-year old 'officer of the Imperial Japanese Army,' and laughed.

"*Ko no Danshi wa bakarashii desu,*" one of them said, "this young fellow is deranged." The others shook their heads, looked down, and walked away. I could have chased after them and asked them more, but then what was the point? If that's what a Kumiko looks like, I'd rather let her re-marry a man like him, skinny and bent, than have her live with me! I managed to console myself.

As I walked along the Esplanade and beside the Singapore river, my mind became suddenly calm and composed after meeting my former countrymen. What's the point? I asked myself. *Here am I, with a new life, born and raised in comfort and in a loving family. I should be grateful and not go looking for my past life and past death.*

I knew I should embrace my life as it was, as native of Syonan To or Singapore, the island that we, the Japanese, so easily conquered from the British, almost without a fight.

I laughed and cried, as I threw a twig from the overhanging Flame of the Forest tree. It landed on the dark and slowly moving waters, amidst the busy churning of the Chinese bumboats that almost choked the river.

"Sayonara, my old country, my Emperor, and Kumiko, or whoever, wherever you are—Sayonara."

I took a slow walk home.

Chapter Five

W hen I finally reached home that day, there was some excitement in the air. Something was going on as I entered the gate. My father's chauffeur was on the driveway, polishing the Mercedes. "Your parents will be home tomorrow," he said, "and Fat Aunt has found her daughter!"

Fat Aunt! Her daughter? Well, after so many years, Fat Aunt had finally made contact with her elder sister, the evil one who'd sold her off to the theatrical group so many years ago. Maybe it was out of remorse or guilt that she let on to Fat Aunt where the long lost daughter might be found.

I entered the house to the sound of happy laughter in one room and tears in another. The daughter cried as she hugged Fat Aunt, the mother she had never known, while the elder sister sat in a corner with tears flowing down her face—tears to wash off what had happened so many years ago.

"Fat Aunt will be leaving us tomorrow," my Gran announced. "She will be living with her daughter from now on."

Thus I was served with another separation, another parting. I stayed silent in a corner until most of those in the room had left, and I was alone with Fat Aunt. She hugged me and said, as though reading my thoughts: "Don't worry, I will still be around whenever you want me. Just remember all that I have taught you," she said, still hugging me. "The three nails, the three bunches of spring onion and the way to read and draw the charms. I will be there."

I was not sure if she would ever be, as I never tried what she taught me to do. After all, Fat Aunt was usually just a holler away in the next room or the kitchen whenever I needed her. But I nodded in agreement.

"Yes, I will do that." I did so just to let her go—a release, a cut to the umbilical cord that had linked me to this special someone who knew of my past and would have been able to help me to chart my future.

"So, I'll never be a Mau San," I said.

"Don't be silly, there are many ways of becoming a Mystic—many schools that will teach you how to reach the top of the mountain. Only different roads. Just stay on the course and—who knows?—one day someone will find you if it is meant to be. Just study hard for your coming exams."

"Fat Aunt," I said, "I have got rid of my past life." She laughed. "How can you? It will stay and surface whenever the time comes for it to. Take it as a blessing that you now have the experience of more than two lifetimes to count on."

"More than two lifetimes?"

"Of course. A soul passes from one lifetime into another, wrapping itself like an onion, with past experiences and memories," Fat Aunt tried her best to explain. "It's just that we are not able to remember our past lives and call on what we had learnt from times past. Most of us, anyway."

She paused for a moment and looked at me. "Not many of us are like you, Ah Jan. If you can calm yourself, you may discover that you had lives, hundreds of them before. Make use of all the experiences you must have had, and maybe, someday, it will be you who will have something to teach us." With that, she brushed her hand on my cheek—a sign of an Oriental saying goodbye.

Rashid, the chauffeur, drove Fat Aunt and her meagre belongings to the daughter's house the next day. I was at school so I did not have the chance to say goodbye. I came home at eight that night. Lei Wah, the elder servant, told me that Fat Aunt had gone into my room, left me a small packet of something, hugged my pillow, and cried before leaving.

I went to my room immediately. As usual, it was in some disarray. My books and files were in a heap on the table, and my spear and my Thai sword, the Dap, in a corner. But I could sense that there was something else, a presence in the room. My bed was made up, but something drew me closer to it. I lifted the pillow and underneath was a small red parcel. I had seen it in Fat Aunt's room before, but never saw what it contained.

I closed the door, laid the parcel on my table and, with trembling hands, unwrapped it. Three rusty long nails, each about nine inches long and wrapped together with a man's braided pigtail—the hair white and tied with red cotton cord. It must have once belonged to her Mau San Master or Sifu. Also in the bundle were seven strips of Chinese paper charms with diagrams once drawn with blood.

What she had left me was all that she had taught me over two years in the late of each night; those incantations, spells and hand movements to draw the charms in the air. What she had left me in that parcel was a badge that I was her disciple, never mind what her own Master had said that night in the banana grove.

That evening, I looked at myself in the mirror. So, I have been trained to be a Mau San, a Chinese Mystic. Would I be strong enough to suffer the trials and tribulations that would come with this new life?

Somewhere outside my window, a dog howled.

Chapter Six

Weeks passed. It was hard for me to contain my excitement, for I was now a trained Mystic. This was one secret that I was more than willing to share. *Young as I am, I am now a Mau San or Chinese Mystic.*

Nosey and Johnny were the two brothers who lived a few houses away from ours. Though we did not go to the same school, we always made it a point to meet under the old jackfruit tree behind their father's garage after school, there to get ready for our daily forage into the belukar or secondary jungle to try our luck with the catapult. Anything that flew was fair game, and I still shudder at the number of innocent birds we brought down.

One day, I mentioned to them that I was now a Chinese Mystic.

"So what can a Chinese Mystic do?" Johnny asked, his eyes

on the ground, looking for a stone for his next kill.

"Well, I can banish Devils, ghosts and whatever spirits. I can bring on strong winds, storms. I can even disappear at will." I went on and on. The list got longer with my telling and I could feel my chest swell at my own importance. The two brothers listened and when I finished, Nosey spoke.

"If you are that powerful," he said, "why don't you try banishing the ghost in that haunted house on the hill?"

"Which house?" I asked.

"That one, with the smashed door and broken windows at the front—the Japs killed a lot of people in that house, that's why it is now haunted."

I felt enraged. We Japanese soldiers only killed when we had to, by order or by necessity. And certainly not in this quiet neighbourhood, something told me. Perhaps I just knew, as I was probably there not so long ago. These natives tend to attribute any haunting to the work of our Imperial Army. I kept my cool and said nothing, half expecting a challenge to come. It did.

"Eh, if you are so powerful," Johnny said, "why don't we meet there tonight and let us see what you can do." I was eager to accept the dare, after all I was keen to see what I could really do with my Mau San training.

There is hardly any twilight time in our part of the world.

At seven thirty in the evening, someone on high just flicks the switch and the world gets dark all of a sudden. The three of us met there at nine that night. I brought my candles, my Mau San wooden sword and a small stack of self-made paper charms.

The door was half ajar as we went in. Using Nosey's torch, we could see that there had been a fire in a corner some time ago. The wall was blackened and there was a pile of sand on the middle of the floor.

A broken chair and some rope were at the other end of the room, and pieces of rags lay strewn around.

"See, that's where the bloody Japs tied and tortured their victims," Johnny said.

"And that is where they probably hung them," Nosey added.

I stayed calm, lit my two white candles and with two fingers drew charms in the air, all the while reciting what incantations I was taught by Fat Aunt. After a while the candles flickered and the room became colder.

"There's someone walking upstairs," Johnny whispered.

"Yes, I can hear him," Nosey said.

I wasn't perturbed and went on with my chanting. I invoked the Masters of the Order of the Mau San. I commanded the good spirits to be of assistance on this my first task. As I chanted deeper into the night, the footsteps above grew louder. Whatever was above started stomping around. We could hear it now, stomping down the stairs.

Toomph! Toomph! Toomp! Toomph! Toomph!

Then silence. Nosey and Johnny got up, holding on to each other, petrified. Just then, one of the candles blew out and something kicked at the adjoining door. Nosey and Johnny ran for their lives, both screaming like a pair of banshees in heat.

I got up from the floor, the remaining candle started sputtering and was ready to go out at any moment. I was no more a teenager now, but an Officer of the Imperial Japanese Army. "*Anata wa watakushi ni unugasu shimasu, watakushi wa O-shi Shoko desu!* —how dare you mess with a Japanese Officer!"

"*Banzai!*" I cried as I charged at the door. Flinging it open, I readied a kick at whatever spirit was hiding in the next room. There was an almighty howl as the spirit made contact with my shoe. It tried to turn and run back into the darkness as my candle finally blew out. I managed to give another kick in the same direction. Another howl of pain followed as I made contact with that thing.

"Sorry! Sorry! *Maàf maàf,*" it pleaded. It was human, an Indian boy whom I had seen around before.

"*Doshita? Baka!*" I shouted in Japanese, for once forgetting about my secret past identity. "*Dameh Daiyo!*" I shouted, slapping him.

"Sorry! Sorry!" he cried again. "Johnny and Nosey put me up to it," he pleaded. His nose was bleeding and his left eye swollen as our candle, now relit, revealed. "Bloody Ramasamy! What are you doing?" I shouted, "I could have killed you."

Almost in tears, Ramasamy accepted my handkerchief and tried to stop the bleeding.

"Johnny and Nosey, they asked me to frighten you," he said again. I let the poor fellow go.

My servants were huddled together in whispers the following morning. From what I could gather, sometime during the night, stones rained down on Nosey's house, followed by piercing devilish screams. His whole family was terrified out of their wits and no one dared sleep.

Nosey and Johnny suspected me, but their father was adamant that it was a ghost and threatened to call on the services of a Mau San.

I knew nothing. I slept the whole night through. I was dead to the world.

Promise!

Chapter Seven

W as I offended at the trick played on me by Nosey and Johnny? No. I enjoyed that night at that 'haunted house'. I became more of myself, that Japanese officer once again, with the training and the pride that came with it, serving the Emperor, who was still very much alive but rendered a mortal by General MacArthur. I was already dead in Burma when He, our Emperor, read out his proclamation of Total Surrender to the Allied Forces after Hiroshima and Nagasaki.

'To bear the unbearable' and lay down our arms. We would have fought to the last man, woman and child had He commanded, but He saw the wisdom to carry on as a nation, for with life, many the outcome of a battle can be reversed.

Are we still at war? On any front? I resolved to grow up stronger as a man, to acquire more powers in order to change things around me. My Mau San training did not help with the faked ghost Johnny and Nosey planted that night. It could well have worked if it were a real ghost. Fat Aunt wouldn't have spent those late nights teaching me things that had no meaning. I kept her parcel of Mau San items safely tucked in a drawer and looked for other things to immerse myself in.

Our final exams over and their results not due for another nine months, I got permission from my parents to travel up north to visit my childhood friend Ah Chee in Perak. The slow lumbering train stopped at Tapah Road, a small station along the North-South railway line. From there I took another to this little town of Telok Anson. Located on the estuary of the mighty Perak River, it boasted a few rows of old Chinese shop houses, a small wharf for steamers ferrying coal, tin and timber out to sea and back with sacks of rice, dried fish and canned goods for the local population.

One of Telok Anson's chief features then was its Leaning Clock Tower, built like a pagoda but, alas, on the soft muddy bank of the river. The locals had long ago given up attempts to halt its tilt. Yet, as long as it stood, it was a constant marvel that it had not yet toppled. A feature to see, marvel at, and then stay clear of.

Chee met me when I got off the train. He had a job as a technician in their telephone exchange. A few years older than I in this life, he was a good friend who accepted me as this clumsy youth who knew everything and yet not how to care for himself. I was still between two worlds—battle sounds and the dying cries of my men at one end of my mind; the quietness of the jungle when we used our catapults on birds at the other. Walking a tightrope between the two worlds, I was often absent-minded and uncaring.

Chee ignored my predicament and carried my bags to his little Morris Minor. He had fried eggs, rice, and fish ready for our main meal when we arrived. He said I was free to do whatever I wanted as long as I did not get myself into more trouble.

"More trouble—?"

"Yes, your father told me about the thrashing you gave a poor Indian kid."

"You mean that fake, that ghost?" I asked. I started to tell him about that episode of our visit to that 'haunted house'. Chee laughed.

"You should have walloped that Johnny and Nosey bunch instead."

"Well, I didn't really wallop them, but stones and gravel kept falling on the roof of their house for days, and now they have moved away, fearing that their house really is haunted now."

"So how many days or nights did you keep up the barrage?"

Chee asked, still laughing.

"Whenever I can't sleep," I said, not telling him that I would have had them beheaded if I were still a Japanese officer.

"Ah, that's terrible!" Chee said.

"Not really. Nosey's father owed six months of rent. I just gave them a good excuse for running away and blaming a ghost for their not paying."

Nosey suspected me, but his father was adamant that it was a ghost, so they had a good reason to leave.

"I suppose that's okay then," Chee nodded, "you helped them."

A Mau San can help in many different ways, so I told myself, and proceeded to attack the fried fish with gusto. Boy, was I hungry after such a long trip. I'd only eaten bananas on the train.

Like all little towns, Telok Anson has its share of visiting mendicants, medicine peddlers and the like. In order to attract a crowd and so its potential customers, there would be a lot of drum and gong-banging, signalling their presence and the promise of a good show. One morning while Chee was at work, I was just loitering around with nothing much to do when the sound of a gong made me follow others to its source.

By then, a small crowd had already formed a circle around this 'medicine peddler'. He was a man of about thirty, well built, with the light brown skin of a Malay. His wares were in little green bottles and in boxes full of more bottles, stacked in a heap. When he surveyed the crowd being thick enough for his show, he started his spiel.

Without the usual 'Pardon me if I make a mistake, after all, I'm here just to earn a small living to feed my family'—an unspoken requirement in all peddlers' etiquettes before they start so as not to be deemed arrogant by any onlooker—this man started his show by saying the opposite.

"Consider yourself lucky," he declared, "that I am here to save you all! Look at him!" he said, picking out a skinny man in the crowd. "And him!" said he, pointing to a pale and gaunt one this time, "men like that can't walk straight, they can't run, not even when their wives are snatched from them." The crowd laughed. He continued picking out and mocking individuals for the crowd's amusement.

"Now just look at me!" he said, flexing his muscles and showing off his biceps. Then, slapping his thigh, he made a leap and a jump, to demonstrate his martial arts skill. "I am this strong because of this special medicine that I take," he boasted, making another leap into the air.

Beside me there stood an old Malay man, dressed in a pair of white pants and shirt and wearing his black songkok—a Muslim cap—and holding a black umbrella in one hand. Together we watched the antics of this peddler for a while. As he went on, the peddler became more offensive and arrogant with each passing minute, deriding more members of the crowd and praising himself to no end. Finally the old man could contain himself no longer, as more men were picked out and ridiculed.

"So you are very strong?" he asked the seller.

"Of course," came the reply.

"Good. You see this green coconut shell on the ground?" the old man said, pointing to a half shell of a green coconut before him. "Just come here and pick it up."

The peddler threw back his head and laughed, strode towards us smiling, bent down, and with one hand, tried to pick up the shell.

Just as he bent down and in front of our eyes, an unseen force pushed him back. The crowd gasped. The peddler stood up, surprised, but still as arrogant. This time, he marched towards us and, with greater force and effort, made a determined grasp at the coconut shell. He was thrown back further, his hand never even touching the ground.

The crowd was silent, surprised at this display of supernatural power. The peddler, now having lost all hope of making a sale and with nothing more to lose, ran towards us and made a dive for the shell.

But before his body could land, a force—even greater than the previous ones—lifted him off the ground, like a kick from the foot of an invisible giant. He was dumped a few feet away, landing on his stack of green bottles, his stack of boxes, and his dreams of making a sale. He just sat there and cried like a child. The crowd stayed for a while, watched him in silence and pity, and drifted away.

The old man turned, looked at me and smiled.

"I suppose you want to learn that too?" he asked.

"Yes!" I said eagerly.

"*Honto desu ka?*" he asked me in Japanese. "Is it true?" He threw his head up and laughed. I was speechless. How could he have known that I was Japanese in my past life?

"Guru! Master!" I said in Malay. "Please accept me as your disciple, your *murid,* your student."

"*Sensei, watakushi wa anata wo no deshi tsutomemasu onegai shimasu, kudasai!*" I blurted in Japanese. I was desperate; I needed to know more. He laughed. "Meet me at the boat pier tomorrow night at ten." He shook his head and, still laughing, walked away.

Left alone in the scorching sun, I felt not the heat, but intense joy at meeting another Master. I went and bought myself a chocolate ice cream before heading back to Chee with the good news.

Chapter Eight

"Chee! You will not believe what has happened."

"I know, I heard the story too, it is all over town" said he in reply. "That was Pak Samad, the old man who did it."

"So you know him?" I asked, surprised.

"Well, he has always been seen as something out of the ordinary, a Mystic or a madman. Depending on whom you ask. No one really knows where he came from."

Chee went to his favourite kitchen chair, the one beside his little aquarium, lit up a cigarette and continued with his story.

"From what little we know of him, and according to what he told us, when he was a young man, he disappeared into the jungle—went missing, shall we say. Despite all attempts to find him, he left without a trace, so the locals presumed him dead, eaten by a tiger or kidnapped by the Communist terrorists, maybe killed or made to work for them.

"But some years later, according to Pak Samad, he emerged unscathed, outwardly anyway, and claimed that he went with a group of *Orang Bunyiaan*—invisible fairy folks—and even married one of their fairest maidens."

"So? What happened?" I asked, unable to contain my curiosity.

"He claimed that despite the wonderful world he was allowed to live in, a land probably of milk and honey, of song and dance, he longed for his village or kampong. He gave them the slip and came back to our world."

"Then what happened?"

"He never was the same, a bit odd. Not the full shilling!" Chee laughed.

"Did you see his shoes?"

"No, I was too engrossed with watching the show."

"You should have. He always wears a black leather shoe on one foot and a white one on the other. Once, thinking that he was too poor and wore any shoe that he could find, I bought him a pair of white ones. Well, he gave me back the left one, saying that it would not fit him and only took the right one!"

I couldn't help laughing.

"So I had to buy him a new pair of black leather ones, of which he promptly wore the left shoe and gave me back the right one!" We both had a good laugh and Chee offered me a cigarette.

"And you are going to meet him tonight?"

"No, tomorrow night at ten, by the jetty," I replied.

I did not dare tell Chee that Pak Samad knew of my past life as a Japanese Officer. Chee could not even remember his father. He was one of the Chinese men rounded up and executed by our Japanese troops as we swept down the Malayan Peninsula on our way to conquer Singapore.

"Be careful," Chee warned. "This guy is queer. God knows what he might do to you. Maybe take you to the Fairies and make you marry one of their ugliest!" he added laughingly.

Our dinner that night was fried salted fish, eggs, rice, and a banana each for dessert. We toasted to a life of 'simple living and high thinking' with black coffee. Only the poor can afford high thoughts, I mused, and poverty is not a crime. There was a show of fireflies by the river that night. We just sat, smoked all our cigarettes, and so ended our day.

Chapter Nine

Chee gave me a tweak on the ear the next morning. "Eh, wake up! I have to go to work and will be back late. You are to clean up the mess in the house, feed my cat if she comes back, the tropical fish, and also water the plants inside. Don't forget!"

I hardly stirred as I heard him drive off in his Morris Minor. I had been dreaming of being back in Burma all night long, fighting the whole British Army. The whites, the black Nigerians, and the Gurkhas. I was hoarse shouting orders to my men, jumping into one trench or fox hole to urge them on.

In one scene, I even led a Banzai charge wielding my samurai sword.

I woke many a time covered with sweat, then fell back to sleep again to dream of more skirmishes with the Teki or enemy. It was a good night for my dreaming, where I killed every bloody one, but a bad night for me when I woke to aching bones and muscle.

Chee's house had three bedrooms, a hall and a kitchen. Since my arrival, we had spent more time messing around and denying the fact that the house needed a good clean. I started with one room, took out the stack of old newspapers and magazines, rehung the pictures on the wall, and swept the floor. In the second and third, I just made our beds and wiped the window panes clean of grime and dead flies.

The hall was the biggest task of all. The chairs—one with his stupid cat's hair on the cushion and one that needed a few more nails to hold it together. The floor I washed and scrubbed clean, and watered his plants, mainly pots of ferns from the jungle, none flowering or meant to. Chee hardly bought anything. We chose to live simply and enjoy life as life wanted us to.

Chee's aquarium was home to a shoal of tiger barbs, which he caught in the stream beside the rubber estate, and clown loaches from the other side of town. With their distinctive red fins and black stripes, I observed them busily foraging for the food I dropped in as I cooked a meal of rice, boiled cabbage and prawns.

With some eight hours to go of the sun blazing down on this sleepy town, I decided to take a walk away from Anson and head into the countryside.

'Marlborough Rubber Estate', the sign read. What a name. It must have had an English owner so many years ago. There were only a few Brits left, what with the low price of rubber and the high murder rate of British Planters by the Communists up and down the country a few years ago.

It had a laterite road, leading all the way in to where the planter's house, and the labourers' quarters would be.

As I walked on, the silence of the place was unsettling. I could hear each of my footsteps on the red gravel and the whine of mosquitoes now that they had found a new food source. Waving them away with little success, I walked on. Stretched out across the road before me was a brown rope, rapidly moving from left to right and heading into the tall unkempt grassy verge.

A snake. Good fun, I thought, as the tail came into view. I picked it up and pulled it along as I walked. The snake was at least ten feet long and was trying to move deeper into the bush. I kept an eye on its struggle to get away, smiling to myself at its efforts. Then it suddenly changed course. Instead of heading deeper into the lallang grass, it made a u-turn and went straight for my leg.

I saw it coming and, just before it could sink its fangs into me, I flipped it up into the air. It landed a few feet from me and rose, its hood expanded for the world to see. A king cobra.

It hissed and spat and swore, its hooded head twisting this way and that, hoping to find a movement anywhere so as to home in and attack. I kept still and recited a mantra that Fat Aunt had taught me. As I chanted, I invoked the Deities to calm a storm—a natural one, a storm in one's mind or even a storm in a teacup.

The king cobra stayed still as I recited the last passage of the prayer, and slowly closed its hood, dropped to the ground and moved away. What a close shave, I thought to myself. One bite and I would be back with my men in Burma!

Evening was fast approaching and in a few minutes, nightfall. I got back to Chee's house, washed and changed and set out to meet my new Master, if he would agree to teach me.

Telok Anson is usually busier at night than day. Market stalls stay open selling food of all kinds. As I walked past the satay stalls and the fried noodles, I wished I had enough money for a plate of each. With only a dollar in my pocket, I bought a bunch of bananas and walked on to the pier to meet my new Master.

The river could be smelt a mile away. Fish and prawn laid out to dry give off a smell that tells you of the sweat of fishermen and the sea. I could hear the gentle lapping of the tide on the boats and the clunk clunks as they came together, with each swell. Pak Samad was there waiting. He must be early I thought. I looked at my watch. It said ten minutes to twelve! What—?

"Pak Samad! I'm sorry I'm late, so, so sorry." I nearly knelt to apologise. God! Could I have been that late? How did time fly so fast?

"No, you are not late," Pak Samad laughed, "we are both early." I looked at my watch again. It now said ten minutes to nine! I was speechless and could just manage to hand him the bunch of bananas—"some little token for you Pak, I am sorry that I couldn't afford more tonight."

He laughed again. "Don't worry, Ah Jan. It is my job to take you as a student."

He even knows my name?

"My name. How, how—?"

"Well, your last Master told me."

"But Pak Samad, my last Master was a woman and she is in Singapore."

"Well, we Mystics live in a different world where there is no space and no time. You proved yourself well this afternoon."

"What? With the snake?"

"Yes, I had to test you, to test your bravery and how well you had been trained," he said. "You had training in the Chinese form of Mysticism, did you not? You chanted well."

"How did you know that I did? Don't tell me that you were that snake?"

"What do you think?" he said, still laughing.

Chapter Ten

We sat on the still warm timbers of the pier and stared at the already dark river for a while. Pak Samad said nothing. I looked at his feet. Yes, he had one black shoe and one white, which was both amusing and strange.

"Pak Samad," I asked, "why the different shoes?"

"Well, I usually wear white when I am in Hari Kong and black when I am amongst you all, but I prefer to be neither here nor there, he said quietly. "The way of the Mystic is seldom understood. You must first die before you can live again, like us. You have died in the real sense so many years ago, but your spirit chose to stay on in this world of men. While others have left and gone on, you returned to fight another war." He paused for a moment before continuing.

"There are no more world wars to fight, my Japanese officer. Japan is at peace with the world. The world is at peace. So, you poor chap," he smiled, "you are left with half of you dead and the other half alive. That is why you can be one of us. All you need is the proper training to be a good Mystic."

"How do you know of my past life?"

"We can 'see'—see what a man is made of, what he was made from, and what he is made to be."

I hoped to ask him more of my past life, my name, rank, and whatever he could tell me, but he held up his hand.

"The more you know of your past, the less you will do with the future. Can you drive a car by looking in the rear view mirror?"

He laughed again.

"As you achieve more power, you will find out more about yourself and realise that what a man was, is of no importance."

"What is this Hari Kong, Pak Samad?"

"Hari Kong, or the Eighth day of a week is a space in time, reserved for Mystics. Most people have only seven days in a week, but we have eight. In our Eighth day, we gather all Mystics and beings of this and not of this world, where we teach and learn and help each other with our problems."

"Hari Kong is the time when we can decide which way the world should unfold for the humans. We can use it to lengthen or shorten a day, so as to cause an event or prevent it from happening. Just like what I did to show you tonight. I stretched time for two hours and then shortened it by one. If a man is to be killed by a car, say at 9pm your time, with our help, that nine o'clock won't come about till he is home safely."

"Pak Samad," I said. "Do you do that all the time?"

"No, only when an event is to cause countless suffering on the innocents and the intended victim had gathered enough good deeds in his life to deserve such support."

Somewhere, a nightbird called.

"Ah, Sri Pelangi is here," he said.

"Where?"

"There!" he exclaimed, pointing with his umbrella. "You can't see her, but I can. See that light?"

There was a fleeting flash of light in the sky.

"*Dia ada, di sini!*" He spoke in Malay. "He is here! Here with me."

A night heron landed on the thick stake of the pier, strutted or maybe danced a step or two and, with her head turned sideways, looked closely at me.

"*Ia, ini lah dia!*—yes, this is he."

"Go, give her a banana!" Pak Samad ordered.

I tore off one from the bunch and walked towards the bird. It stayed still as I left the fruit on the jetty floor. Gingerly, she picked up the banana with her beak and flew away.

"Ah, a good omen. She approves of you. She likes you. It means that you can now follow me to meet the others soon."

"Soon? How soon?"

"In our time, our time, my little Jepun."

Jepun is Malay for Japanese. It was really getting late and we had finished eating the whole bunch of bananas while sitting on the pier. The air had now turned cold.

"Time to go," Pak Samad said, getting up. "*Nak buah buah lagi?*—want more fruits?" Laughing, he opened the umbrella over his head, folded it and then opened it again this time with the tip pointing down.

There were fruits of all kind in that umbrella. Even in the dark, I could see mangoes, apples, pears, and even a pineapple.

"Go on," he said, "take off your shirt, use it as a basket and take these fruits home."

Never had I seen such magic before. I did as I was told. The buttoned shirt was now inverted to form a bag for the fruits, which I slung on my back; dressed only in my singlet and pants, I turned to thank him.

Pak Samad was nowhere to be seen.

Chapter Eleven

It was almost one in the morning when I reached Chee's place. A surprise was waiting for me. Instead of Chee's house being in darkness and he asleep, his house and those of his neighbours were ablaze with all lights on. A small crowd of neighbours had gathered outside Chee's house and there was animated chatter all round.

I hastened my pace, dropped the fruits at the base of the steps and rushed in looking for Chee.

"What happened?" I shouted.

"*Perompak!*—robbery!" said one of his neighbours.

Chee was slumped in a chair, bleeding from a parang or machete wound to his arm. It wasn't too deep, but enough to show a glimpse of the humerus, and blood was still seeping out from the gash.

"What happened?" I shouted again at everyone. "Chee!" I

cried, turning to him, "are you badly hurt?"

"They rushed into one house after another," Chee replied, "three of them, slashing with their parangs as they gathered whatever they could lay their hands on and moved on."

I could see my friend was drained of all strength and still in shock. I managed with the help of Samy, his neighbour, to put a proper bandage over Chee's arm.

"It will hurt, no doubt, but we will get help soon," I said.

Another neighbour produced a few tablets of sulphadiazine, a left-over from a former prescription. "Take that Chee, it should help."

Chee managed to get up from his chair, walked into a room and motioned me to come along. When we were alone, he leaned on my shoulder and cried.

"They took my Father's watch."

I knew that watch meant the world to him. It was the only thing his father had left behind when our soldiers came to take him and others away for execution.

"Don't worry, Chee, I will get it back for you!" I said with full confidence but also with some sadness. "I will get it back, OK?"

"But how?" He looked up at me, with tears still streaming down from his eyes—tears of pain and tears for the loss of his watch.

"Just wait," I said as I lowered him on his bed to rest, "we will be back."

I came out of the house to the small crowd of chattering men. Five huddled in an excited group with one Malay constable, taking notes.

"How many of them were there?" I shouted, "and which way did they go?"

They pointed towards the rubber treeline. There had been three robbers—two Indians and one Malay, all three armed with parangs.

"Follow!" I said, motioning to the one with the torch, and went ahead. It did not take us long to find their footprints and that was all I needed.

"Let's go back and get some nails!" I ordered. Back in the compound, I sent the men scurrying to look for nails. "The longer the better!" I shouted out.

"How many do you need?" one asked.

"The more the better!" I said. I could see the womenfolk peeping out of their windows more frightened by my countenance that the recent robbery.

"Go on, be quick!" I shouted again, my voice reverting to that of a Japanese Officer. "*Hayaku!*"

It was Samy who found the bundle of six-inch nails.

"Will these do?" he asked, afraid of everything that had happened and now this stranger who could suddenly bark orders with a Japanese accent that would send grown men running. I took the nails and went back to Chee's house after ordering the men to wait outside.

It is Mau San time, I told myself. Mau San's payback time! Sadness filled my soul at the coming goodbye, but it was time that I helped my good friend. I sat at Chee's coffee table, in the light of two white candles, laid out a few sheets of white paper and started my chanting and then as I did, drew a few charms on the paper. With the ritual complete, I walked down the steps towards the men.

"Follow!" I ordered. We went to where the footprints were and I motioned the others to stay away. I hammered six nails into each pair of footprints, three to each foot, burned the paper charms and, when complete, stood up and motioned the men to come along. The five men, all with their parangs and the constable with his truncheon, followed me in silence. As we went deeper into the rubber plantation with two men lighting the way, we could see evidence of the robbers' passage. The dried leaves showed a trail leading deeper into the dark.

We went on in silence as I led. It wasn't hard to track them for, after a while, we could see blood stains along their way. There was evidence of them sitting on the ground and fresh blood on the dry leaves. And of someone trying to crawl on fours.

"*Alamak*—oh God!" said one of our men, looking at me in awe. "What happened?"

"Keep going," I said, avoiding the question. "We will not have long to go."

Some hundred yards or so, the sound of distress could be heard.

"*Adoi! Sakit! Tolong, tolong!*—Ow! The pain! Help, help!"

I laughed as our torches showed up the three men, sitting together and in shock to see their feet bleeding, each foot with three holes gushing blood. It did not take us long to apprehend them and recover their loot. I just wanted Chee's watch back and left the others to sort out the scoundrels.

I walked back to Chee's house, retrieved the fruits and went in to see him. Chee was half asleep for it was almost four in the morning.

"Chee, here's your father's watch," I said, handing it back.

He jerked up, too surprised for words.

"Ho? How?" was all he could say.

"Ah, just lucky that's all. By the way, Chee, I will have to leave in the morning."

"Where to, Ah Jan?" he asked.

"Any old where," I replied. "Any old where."

Such are the rules of the Mau San. If you have done 'good' and helped someone, you must not stay for applause or reward.

If you have done 'bad', you must stay until the mistake is corrected or the misunderstanding cleared. That is why we are never 'rich' or famous, and that is why we still exist.

I turned in and slept a dreamless night.

Chapter Twelve

I woke at ten the next morning. Chee had been up and about before me, and despite his wound he was rather cheery. Wearing his father's watch and swearing never ever to put it down on the kitchen table again, he smiled as he made our pot of coffee.

Our breakfast consisted of various cakes and delicacies sent over by his neighbours as a gesture of thanks for our help in apprehending the three robbers.

Not long after our second cup of coffee, there was a knock on the door. A crowd had assembled outside, all wanting to meet me, the magic man who had performed such a feat, the like of which they had not seen or heard of before. Chee told them that I would be out to meet them after my breakfast. The neighbours agreed to wait on the steps and prevent the crowd from the town from forcing their way up to see me.

"Ah Jan, where and when did you learn these magic tricks?" Chee asked casually. "Why have you not told me?"

"I learnt it from a book," I lied.

"Come on! From a book? Which book?"

"Lobsang Rampa's," I said.

"That fellow is a bloody fake! He is a Welshman and not a Tibetan as he claimed." he laughed. "Come on, tell me. Who taught you?"

I proceeded to tell him about our Fat Aunt. Chee listened for a while, but a commotion outside the house interrupted my story.

"The police are here! What do they want now?" Chee came back from the window. "Look, the crowd is getting bigger!"

I could see that my friend was feeling uncomfortable.

"What shall we do?" he asked me.

"Don't worry Chee, I will be leaving soon."

"How are you going to? Are you going to hop out of the window?"

"Something like that," I said. "Just let me pack up my things and I'll be gone. By the way, Chee, it was nice to see you after all these years, and thanks for the hospitality."

"Forget it, chum. You are welcome anytime." Still looking at the gathering crowd outside, Chee looked at me now more worried than ever. "Can't they just leave us alone?"

I went into my room, with the door closed, tied the haversack on my back and prepared for my departure from Telok Anson the Mau San way. I had to leave, to disappear before the crowd of curious onlookers came crashing into Chee's home and his peace.

I could see faces bobbing up and down at my window, trying to catch a glimpse of me.

There was no time to waste. I recited the spells that Fat Aunt taught me not so long ago, and tried to picture the place where I wanted to be. My mind flickered from one scene to the next, but, with the commotion outside and the confusion in me, I could not hold on to a picture of any place for long. Scenes of my own home, my school, my friend Robin's house, and the Botanical Gardens in Singapore came and went, never staying still long enough for me to home in.

I could hear Chee knocking at the door.

"Ah Jan! Are you alright?" he asked.

"I'm ok, I'm fine!" I said.

Then I thought of Tapah Road, that little sub-station with the jungle behind. That scene somehow stayed in my mind. That was good enough. I kept focused on that scene and cleared all other thoughts. Reciting the sacred Mau San verses, I made the appropriate signs with my hands, my fingers entwined into one configuration and then another.

Three claps—one! two! three!—and before I knew it, I was travelling past a wall of smooth pastel pink and could feel the buzzing of time and space that I was moving through. I then fell out of whatever carried me into the bright sunshine and into the belukar behind the station. I staggered up, feeling very sick and dizzy. I had to throw up—blood, fresh blood, into the nearby bush and staggered on along the railway track.

"Oi!" a shout from behind made me look back. It was from the Indian station master. "*Oi! Awak Mabok ka?*—Are you drunk?" And then: "*Gila punya orang! Mana lu mahu pergi?*" he added in bazaar Malay—"mad fellow, where do you think you are going?"

I just waved back at him and walked on. I needed to relieve myself; I needed to pee. I staggered into the confines of a bush and did so. Again, it was fresh blood. I felt faint and just let myself fall on the belukar, ignoring the sharp twigs, the thorns and all.

I am not sure how long I lay there. It was late afternoon, close to five in the evening, when I regained consciousness. I looked around me, the railway track still in front and the setting sun casting early shadows on a warm evening. From the corner of my eye, I could see something emerge from the bush beside me. A small head with a red comb, then his feathers of red, orange, green, gold—a jungle rooster, dressed in the most flamboyant of plumage. It came towards me, unafraid of my presence and started pecking and scratching the ground between my feet.

Strange! It then looked up at me and made a clucking sound. "*Kut, kut. Kut, kut.*"

I smiled at this brave bird—one snatch of my hand and it would be dinner for me. It did not move but scratched even harder at the patch of earth, this time his clucking sounded different. More like "*Ikut, ikut, ikut!*" and with greater urgency. Ikut is 'Follow!' in Malay. *Ikut! Ikut!* He turned and with his head beckoned me to follow. Walking ahead and turning back once awhile to see if I did. "*Ikut! Ikut!*"

Well, I had seen Sri Pelangi, the night heron of Pak Samad, so I supposed this was another Mystic manifestation. *What have I to lose and who is there to laugh at me following a chicken?* Still feeling weak, I roused myself and walked behind this jungle fowl.

"*Ikut, ikut,*" he called as he led me up to a narrow jungle track.

I followed him for a few hundred yards until I could see a small pondok or jungle hut built on stilts, under the trees.

Pak Samad and two other men were sitting on the rungs of the ladder, smoking their puchok daun cigarettes. Pak Samad lifted his umbrella and called out.

"Si Jan, Jepun! Come, come, join us."

As I walked towards the men, I felt a darkness envelope me and could see stars all around and felt the weakness in my legs.

Two pairs of hands gripped me and helped me towards the still smiling Pak Samad.

"*Bawak lah Daun Sireh,*" he ordered. I was then given a wrapping of betel nut in the green sireh leaf and was asked to chew. The pungent and bitter taste of the sireh brought me back to my senses. I could feel the warmth returning to my body and a calmness settling in.

"You could have died you know, Si Jan, trying this disappearing act," Pak said. "You could have died. You were too quick to perform what you were taught by your Chinese Master."

"I vomited fresh blood," I said.

"Yes, and you passed fresh blood too," Samad added.

I was too exhausted to ask if he was that bloody rooster in the bush. I just nodded.

"To leave, to disappear, you must summon your physical body and your soul to leave together. Your soul left Telok Anson first, and your spiritual and then your physical self tried to catch up later. This separation of mind, body and soul is the cause of you being so sick.

"You could have died, if the three did not meet up again at the same time. You were saved by just a few seconds. Thank God you came together in time, with only a slight loss in blood. Next time, be careful," he added, helping me down.

Night was already descending, and together with it, the sounds of the jungle.

"This man here is Mat Hijau, and this his student Rahim," Pak said, as he introduced them to me.

"This young man Si Jan is my student," he said, pointing at me. "The one I told you about. Jepun!" he laughed.

Mat Hijau smiled as he held my shoulder.

"*Baik lah,* Good, he can stay here with us till you come back," he said to Pak Samad.

"Jepun! Will you be alright staying here with them, and learn something while you are here?" Pak said, confident that I'd be willing to, and maybe learn something. Learn what? I dared not ask, but just nodded my agreement and thanked my new host and his student.

"Right, I must go! *Nak buah buahan?*—want more fruits?" he asked, laughingly, shaking his umbrella.

"No, no, we don't eat fruits here!" Mat Hijau hastened to tell him.

"Only meat eh? Only meat!" Pak Samad said as he walked down the track. "And maybe fish? And frogs?" He laughed even louder as he disappeared into the dark.

Chapter Thirteen

The jungle can be cold at night. Never mind being in the tropics and all that, when the dew descends and when the warmed earth sends it up back again, its evaporation brings down the cold, or that was my explanation to Rahim, Mat Hijau's student.

I was given a place inside the door to sleep and Rahim slept on the other side of the open door. Mat Hijau sat at the back of the pondok, still smoking his puchok. He took out a small oil lamp and teased its wick and lit it. The flame, the size of a birthday candle on a cake, glowed to life. I could smell the coconut oil as it burned.

Mat asked me about my home and Singapore. Was it a big country? Were there many people there? Were the British still there?

"I've only heard of Singapore," he said, "but I've never been anywhere except to the States of Pahang and Kelantan, to catch wild elephants when I was young, following my father, who was a good elephant tracker. And later, after he was killed by a cobra, I stayed on in the jungle that bordered the State of Trengganu."

"Why?" I asked him. "Why did you not come out into the city to look for a job instead?"

"Ah, I decided to stay and learn *Ilmu* or Magic from my Masters, the Mystics." His voice came from the back of that little room.

As the night grew darker, the little lamp seemed to be about to flicker and die. I could still make out his dark shadow and his face whenever he pulled on his cigarette.

"Masters?" I asked again.

"Yes, Si Jan, your Pak Samad was one of them."

"How old is Pak Samad, Pak Hijau?" I asked.

"Pak Samad?" He laughed. "Older than the mountain. My grandfather was his student, that will show you how old."

Rahim stirred, and sat up.

"Would he be about a hundred?" he asked.

"Maybe three hundred, maybe five, who knows?"

I did not dare ask more, but kept as quiet as the room. Outside I could hear the hoot of an owl then the 'Tok tok' of a nightjar and the splash of something big as it took to the water.

"What was that?" I asked.

"Maybe Kijang the barking deer, or Tenuk the tapir," Rahim offered.

"Maybe Pak Belang," added Mat Hijau. And they both laughed and called it a night.

"Sleep, enough talk," Mat Hijau said.

Pak Belang is the Malay honorific title for the Tiger—'Uncle Stripes'.

Our pondok has no door, and now I am told that there may be a tiger outside. God! What was I in for, I wondered, as I lay down on the grass mat for the night.

I had a fitful night; it felt as though each and every mosquito or bug of the jungle had called to pay their respects. I woke just before the dawn broke. The morning mists lingered in the darker reaches, saying their long goodbyes before the sun broke out and shooed them away. Rahim woke not long after and Mat Hijau was nowhere to be seen. I sat up, shivering, hugging myself and feeling self-pity.

"There is a stream down the slope," Rahim pointed towards a spot further down, "we get our water upstream and bathe further down."

"Do we have soap and a towel?" I asked.

"What soap Si Jan? *Mana ada towel, pulak?*" he smiled. "We

are too poor for these things."

"We use the river sand for soap and our sarong will be enough to dry us as we watch our washed clothes dry in the sun."

And so I started my apprenticeship with Mat Hijau and learnt the meaning of austerity. The fine river sand was a better cleaner than the Palmolive soap we used at home, and stripped of all our clothes, the cold stream made us scrub even harder, faster and better.

Our washed clothes laid out to dry on the bushes, the two of us with our sarongs wrapped around our shoulders, squatted on the bank and watched the dragonflies go by.

"*Eh, Rahim, Ikan Aruan!*" I pointed to a sizeable fish, a snakehead, as it moved slowly in search of smaller fry.

"That's nothing, wait till you see the ones we'll catch in the bigger river," Rahim said as he yawned.

The morning was still young as we walked home. I could see smoke from our pondok. Mat Hijau came out of the door and beckoned us in.

"*Ayoh, makan pagi!*— Come breakfast!" he laughed and Rahim joined in his laughter. We each had three sections of a boiled tapioca root, washed down with hot water. That was our breakfast. No coffee and no sign of sugar. Forget about white bread, fried eggs, jam or cake.

What a life had Pak Samad dropped me into? Yet I was happy. I knew I was on another adventure.

"Ah today, since Si Jan is here to help us," Mat Hijau said as he rolled his daun puchok, "we will go again in our search for the Spirit of Cane."

I could see Rahim with downcast eyes, not too happy with the suggestion.

"We tried really hard on the last few attempts, and it managed to escape us; maybe this time, with Si Jan around, it may be different."

He pushed the tray towards me, containing a packet of red Chinese tobacco cut finer than a human hair and a bundle of dried young palm frond to be unrolled and rolled up again to contain the tobacco. The cigarette, so made, is standard fare for village folks throughout the Peninsula. A social pastime whenever people meet. Smoking the rokok puchok, the same humble cheap tobacco—with no expensive cigarette brands on display—brings about a shared togetherness that we are one and equal.

I was pleased and chuffed when I heard Pak Samad and now Mat Hijau call me Si Jan, and not Ah Jan. I felt they had elevated me to a station higher than a 'Mr.' I took a pinch of the red tobacco and spread it on the unrolled dry leaf, then rolled it back again. I lit my rokok, no more than a third the thickness of an ordinary cigarette, and joined him. 'Si Jan' was a bit of a title, a small measure of respect from my peers and that, for me, outshone any medal.

Rahim got up and went to boil the rice. Mat Hijau took out a few pieces of salted fish from a pot and gave it to him.

"Fry these well, till they're crisp," he ordered while rolling himself another smoke.

'Spirit of Cane' was a term I'd heard Rashid, my father's chauffeur mention before, but I never knew what it was. I was intrigued to say the least.

"What is it?" I asked Rahim.

"I have never seen it either, but we will know once we catch one," he replied, swishing the rice in the pot with water. "This should be enough for the few days in the jungle."

"Few days?"

"Yes, we will be gone for at least five or more. Do you think it is easy?" he added now looking at Mat Hijau, his Master. Mat Hijau smiled as he tied a parang to his waist. Rahim did likewise with his and I followed suit. A parang or jungle machete could be a life saver for anyone wielding it.

Mine had a thick, sixteen-inch long blade, forged and ground from the steel taken from the spring of an old truck, and honed to be as sharp as our katana or samurai sword. Capable of hacking through buffalo bone or a jungle thicket, a parang also serves as a chopper of vegetables or even a pencil sharpener. Such a weapon always obeys the hand that wields it.

I had no idea what was to come, but I could feel the excitement building up in Rahim too as he fanned the wood stove to make the rice cook faster.

"Spirit of Cane? *Apa lah dia pulak?*—What on earth is that?" I asked the two of them. Mat Hijau just smiled and stroked his straggly beard and then his long, matted hair.

"*Si Jan, sabar, Si Jan*—be patient!"

God! What was this Spirit of Cane?

Chapter Fourteen

The rice now finally boiled and the salted fish fried crisp, both the room and our clothes stank.

"Good to keep wild animals away, no more jungle smells," Mat Hijau said without being asked. "Rahim, you take the rice pot and, Si Jan, you take the four bottles of water in that canvas bag and I will take the spear."

Those days, plastic bottles were still very far away and four glass bottles of water were heavy. I lugged the bag over my little haversack that only contained a change of clothes, a sarong and a box of matches.

Mat Hijau had his load, his bag contained as far as I could see packets of benzoin or our own jungle frankincense, a few spikes of metal and a roll of red string and his sarong and a few other items of clothing.

Though his hair was long, matted and unkempt, he wore

his tattered but clean shirt and pants of khaki with pride. That was his old uniform when he worked in Pahang as an elephant trapper so long ago. He stuck his head out of the pondok. It was almost noon.

"Right! Off we go!" he announced.

We climbed down the ladder and went in the direction that Mat Hijau pointed with his parang.

"That way, we must move fast and be there before nightfall," he ordered.

Cane comes from the rattan plant or creeper. Most of us have had contact with it sometime or other, usually with our soft behind when sitting on a chair made of it, while those of a lesser fate made contact with a cane in a more violent manner, delivered by someone who deemed himself or herself one's superior. I have, in my youth, made its acquaintance with my behind many a time, so many times that I want very little to do with it, ever.

Rattan is a jungle creeper that can grow up to more than a hundred feet. With leaves like a palm tree, it ascends to the top of the forest canopy by using the thorns on its bark—sharp black needles, each some two inches long—that can tear the clothes or flesh of the negligent traveller moving through its cluster.

The jungle has many dangers other than animals that we know

of. The tiger, the wild elephant, the seladang or Malayan gaur, snake, and scorpion, but there are a host of other insects and poisonous plants that are there to make life very uncomfortable to an unseasoned traveller.

My experience in the jungles of Burma kicked in. I remembered the impenetrable jungle, the mud and the slime that my men had to move through. The baying of mules and even the hiss and grunt of the elephants used to transport our heavy guns. Those flashbacks, though rare these days, were a help as I followed my two companions deeper into this green tropical morass of Malaya. I had done all that some twenty years ago. Somewhere. But where? I still could not remember.

"We will try capturing it in that big clump of rattan," Hijau said, pointing with his parang.

We moved faster as we could feel the silence and the cooling of the sun's rays. It would be evening soon and then night would fall without warning. We reached the designated area, a dark and wet ground where a big clump of rattan grew—their black thorns sharp and threatening, their stems soaring right to the top of the neighbouring trees, and their leaves spreading on the top of the jungle canopy. In the darkness of the forest floor, few things could thrive save for some fungus amongst the rotting leaves. Home of scavengers like the two-inch long ants, the millipedes, and their more poisonous cousin, the centipede.

Mat Hijau wasted no time in preparing the 'Mystic fence'. Chanting his magic verses to invoke the forest spirits for protection, he circled the grove of rattan and hammered down his iron spikes. These he encircled with red string—his 'pagar' or Mystic fence that no malign spirit can enter. He then called us together into the fence.

"You, Rahim, are to sit here," he indicated a spot on the ground, "and you, Si Jan, there. I will be here and I will keep an eye on you two. Remember, whatever happens, whether you see things that frighten you, hurt you or attract you, you must not move a muscle. Stay still till I tell you to do otherwise. Divide the food into three portions, the rice and the fish and each a bottle of water only. Leave one for an emergency under that tree. Remember, do not panic and do not move."

"Are we to spend the night, without a fire or tent, and each on our own?" I asked.

"Well, you have your parangs, your sarongs for a blanket or tent, that's all you need and it won't rain for a few nights, I know," Mat Hijau said confidently.

I was not afraid and would happily die again, just to find out what was this thing called the 'Spirit of Cane'. I sat on my own, wrapped in my sarong covered to my neck to keep out the insects and the cold. I supposed the other two were doing the same. In the dark a few hours later, I could hear footsteps of a man moving behind me. They stopped and went on again towards where Rahim would be sitting.

It must be Mat Hijau I said to myself, but a cough from his direction alerted me that those footsteps belonged to someone or something else.

I had no torch, and I had been ordered to do nothing but to sit tight. The footsteps came back towards me; someone was standing just behind my back and breathing rather heavily. I stayed still for what must have been twenty minutes, maybe more, as this thing moved, shifting from one leg to another.

Sometime later in the night I heard the soft voice of a woman singing. It came closer and closer to me. Someone bent down to where I was sitting and tried to sing in my ear. I looked on straight—I knew it wasn't human as I did not hear any footsteps. It just floated along as it sang.

With no fear or response from my side, the 'thing' moved away and as she did, there was the sound of her laughter high up in the trees.

Morning came, I had slept not a wink. I ate some of the rice and fish and had a sip of water. Mat Hijau came by.

"Bad night wasn't it?" he said. "That was an Hantu or ghost

last night, hoping to scare us away from our task. We must be resolute, and stay as you are."

"Where can I pee?" I asked.

"Behind that bush, but never inside the fence."

That being cleared, I felt more at ease. I could see Rahim through the trees. He was helping himself with the rice and fish too.

It must have been about four in the afternoon of the second day. I was almost falling asleep when suddenly there was a shrill sound of something coming towards us. Much like an incoming artillery shell. I jumped up and looked towards Hijau.

"*Jaga! Jaga!*—Keep awake! Be on guard!" he shouted.

Whatever it was that had made the sound crashed into the clump of rattan. Mat Hijau jumped into that protected space and as quick as lightning whipped out his parang. He struck at the base of one of the rattan stems that was quivering, as though it had a life of its own.

"Quick, help!" was all he could yell.

The two of us jumped in and tried to help him hold on to one end of the shaking cane while he hacked at a point further up the stem. That done, he had this length of old rattan that was still twisting and turning as though it was trying its best to wriggle free. He chanted in an old Malay or even Khmer dialect, the meaning of which, I could only guess.

"Now tie the red string at each end," he ordered, "and be quick!"

I managed to find it in his bag. Two lengths, each about a foot long of red cotton. I tied as fast as I could a knot at each end of the still quivering stick. What was all this, I wondered. I was sweating and trembling with the excitement. Rahim, probably tutored in this ritual before, brought out the benzoin incense and had it smoking in no time. The cane stopped quivering as Mat Hijau ran it over the benzoin smoke.

"Frankincense from Arabia won't work," he said, when he calmed down. "It must be our own benzoin from the jungle."

Recitations of more sacred and secret verses continued as Rahim and I stayed silent and watched.

"Now, we have the Spirit of Cane," Mat Hijau smiled. "We have it here." He pointed to the stick. Without saying more, he took out his parang and slit the stem open, lengthways. There in the middle was a small piece of what looked like petrified wood or just a piece of coal. He broke it into three parts.

"Nah, one for you, Si Jan, this for you, Rahim, and one for me," he said. "Keep it well."

"All this for a small piece of coal?" I said, forgetting myself as I tucked it into my pocket.

As Mat Hijau turned to look at me, his countenance took a sudden change. I looked into his eyes, they were no longer dark but fast turning yellow! Rahim knew what was coming and tried to get up but he was not fast enough. Mat Hijau swung his parang and cut him on the left shoulder, than slashed again at his back as he tried to dive away.

Now his blade came straight at me as I tried to get up and run for my life, but I was also too late. The parang hit my left arm and as I got up and ran, he managed to slash me again and again twice on my back and the last one just at the base of my neck.

He stopped and shouted.

"Run any further and you will not find your way home!" He laughed and went back to pack up our belongings for the return trip.

I stopped running and, though the cuts hurt like hell, there was neither blood, gash, nor wound. Rahim walked back too. Looking at me and then at his Teacher in amazement.

"No blood—?" was all he could say.

"Of course," Mat Hijau replied without even looking up at us. "You have the Spirit of Cane now, nothing can hurt you," he said while stubbing out the still smoking benzoin. "The two of you are now 'Orang Kebal', Invulnerable Beings," he added with a smile.

Chapter Fifteen

F lushed with the success of our first adventure, we started our return journey when it was getting dark. We walked all those miles in darkness, by just following Mat Hijau.

"My Tok Guru can see everything in the dark," Rahim declared rather proudly, Tok Guru being title for a Grand Master. I call him Pak Hijau when addressing him as a form of respect. Pak stands for either uncle or a fatherly figure. Mat Hijau just kept silent and led the way, faster than we could walk in broad daylight.

This man just moved like a wild animal, ducking occasionally under creepers or overhanging branches that only he could see and stepping over fallen logs and bypassing swampy puddles.

"*Awas Jaga!*—Take care!" was all he said as he led us on.

There was just enough starlight for me to see his form in front, and for Rahim to follow mine from behind. I was about to drop with exhaustion when our pondok came into view.

"*Penat sangat,*" I said. "I'm extremely tired," and gulped from the remaining bottle of water.

"You have to develop more stamina, Si Jan. Life can be tough and no one knows what awaits." Pak Hijau said, sitting himself down on the first rung of the ladder. He took out his puchok and what was left of the tobacco, and rolled himself a cigarette, offering me a smoke. I declined and thanked him.

"This 'Spirit of Cane' is a powerful object to have. It will make you impervious to metal, drive away evil spirits, and protect you from all sorts of dangers."

"What type of dangers?" Rahim asked. "Maybe dangerous women!" Pak Hijau answered. That joke was a welcome release for the tension and stress that we'd felt over these few days. We had achieved our objective and returned home safely. I was first up the ladder and into the hut. Although it was still early, I was totally exhausted and dropped off into deep sleep, too tired to even dream.

I woke sometime in the middle of the night. Rahim was beside me, stretched out, and his face turned in my direction. I could see his features vaguely as there was a shaft of moonlight through the doorway. But I sensed something else was astir in the darker confines of the room. Must be Mat Hijau, I guessed, and stayed still. I had no wish to wake or engage anyone in conversation at that time of the night.

A form, larger than any man, gradually emerged from the shadows and came nearer to me and the sleeping Rahim. It stopped and looked in my direction and slowly turned to look at Rahim before moving down the ladder.

I had never been so shocked in my life, in this life or the one before in Burma, for—descending the steps of the pondok— was a full grown tiger!

The moonlight revealed his stripes of dark brown against a shimmering background of silvery yellow. They would be almost black against orange if he were seen in daylight. He was large, as big as the largest tiger from the State of Pahang.

I nudged Rahim awake.

"*Eh Rahim, Pak Belang di sini!*—Uncle Stripes here!" I whispered.

I am to this day unsure whether Rahim knew what I said or just managed an answer in his sleep when he just mumbled, "go back to sleep, it's just my Tok Guru gone hunting."

From the doorway, I watched the passage of this huge animal, the moon lighting his way. He took his time walking down the slope, went into the bushes and emerged again up the other slope. He then walked a bit further, stopped and turned, looked back at our pondok, entered the jungle and was gone, out of sight.

I sat for awhile at the doorway and looked at the moon and at myself. I felt a wave of sadness descending. *What am I doing with these natives, when I should be back home in Japan? It is near cherry blossom time and the Boy's Festival in May will soon follow.*

I could still remember the streamers of coloured carp flying over every household that boasted a boy, and the little toys of Samurai displayed beside the Tokonama.

I could vaguely remember a ceremony for Officers at the Yasukuni Shrine before we went out to war and how we faced the Emperor's Palace and shouted 'Banzai!' to wish Him a long life.

A night bird flew across the moonlit sky and I was transported back to my present existence—this young fellow being treated to sights that no Japanese would ever get to see. So resigned I was, once again, to see this life through and see where it would take me.

Am I among a pair of 'were tigers'? There were tales of 'were foxes' or 'spirit foxes' in Japan, but I knew nothing about these strange transformations of men into tigers before. Then I remembered seeing Mat Hijau's eyes turn from black to yellow before he hacked us with his parang in the jungle. Was he a 'were tiger'?

Looking up, I could see a halo around the moon.

Chapter Sixteen

After the excitement of the previous night, I woke up in my own sweet time. Rahim and Mat Hijau were busy skinning a deer under the pondok.

"Come Si Jan, help us with the chopping," Rahim shouted. "Guru speared a deer last night and I'll be off to Telok Anson. If you want, you can come too!"

I had never seen a happier Rahim. He was normally quiet, only speaking when it was his turn. I came down the steps and wished them a good morning. Pak Hijau nodded, saying nothing. By then, they had managed to hack the two hocks of the sambar deer with their parangs, leaving the skin intact so as to leave less space for the flies. These hind legs were then strung to each end of a pole, ready for Rahim to carry on his shoulders for his trip to Telok Anson.

"There will be the money to buy what we need here!" Rahim

announced joyfully. "I'll bring back coffee, sugar and coconut oil, and even a bar of soap!"

"Don't forget the rice and the salt fish, and the prawn paste and chillies," Mat Hijau added, laughing while looking at me.

I stayed still and tried to keep my eyes on the ground. I could feel the tension between Hijau and me. There was a sense of uneasiness, of words yet unsaid. I helped with the dismembering of the upper part of the carcass. The head of the animal and the neck was nowhere to be seen. The entrails were present, but I could see the liver was missing as though it had been ripped away and eaten.

"We will sell the two hocks and keep the rest for ourselves. Si Jan, will you get the pot up in the pondok, bring it down and we can do the cooking here." Pak Hijau said. "There is also an old cigarette-tin with the curry powder in it."

I obeyed at once and went up the steps and through the doorway. The pot was easy to find—I supposed it was the big one in the corner beside the doorway not far from where Rahim slept. The cigarette-tin with the curry powder? There were a few tins, all with covers on, so the quickest way was to sniff each one in turn.

Oblivious to where I was standing and only occupied with the tins, I found myself facing the back wall of the hut and, in the broad daylight, I spotted Mat Hijau's spear. I reached out and touched the blade. It was bone dry. It had not been used for a long time, unoiled, unwashed, and certainly it had not tasted blood since I knew not when. I recoiled from it, found the right tin and brought it down to the waiting men.

Rahim was beside himself with the excitement of the trip: "I'll have to walk down to the railway track and then catch the train to Anson from Tapah Road. I should be back tonight!"

"Make sure you don't lose yourself in that joget hall! Don't forget, those joget dancing girls are all married and their husbands watch as their wives dance with you."

"Alamak, can I not just pay for one dance?" Rahim joked. Mat Hijau threw a coconut shell at him and we all laughed as it hit him on the head.

"Don't worry. Look at us." Hijau said. "Who wants to dance with such poor men?"

"Sell these to that Chinese restaurant at the same price as before, and if they refuse to buy, then go on to the butcher in the market, the Chinese one. The Indian one will try to cheat you with his hard luck stories, be careful."

Rahim nodded, with the pole over his shoulder and the two hocks one at each end, as he started his journey to Anson turning back to give us a wave and a smile. It was near noon when we began to cook the venison—cut into small pieces, fried in the curry powder and then boiled in thick coconut milk. What was left after a few hours was a dish called rendang, no gravy, just well-seasoned, dry meat that could be kept for weeks. It was staple fare for sailors in days gone by.

As I stirred the contents of the pot, Mat Hijau looked at me and smiled.

"You saw me last night, didn't you?"

I nodded.

"Well, were you not afraid?"

"No, not really," I answered. I could remember shooting a tiger somewhere before, in my past life. Was it in the jungles of Thailand or Burma? Whatever, I know that a tiger is easy prey for a good hunter.

"We are the Tiger people from Korinchi, we are. We were from Sumatra. Your people made it hard for us to live amongst them and blamed us for every tiger's kill. So we had to move where we could not be found."

"Why do you have to turn into tigers?" I asked.

"We don't want to, if we can help it. But it comes upon us suddenly, especially when we are angry or excited.

"But what was there to excite you last night?" I asked.

"The full moon and the hunger within."

"Can anyone—can I—become one of you? Turn into a tiger?"

Mat Hijau laughed.

"No, you have to be born into our tribe. You have killed one of us before, in your last life," he added, taking the ladle from me and giving the meat a stir.

"How do you know? "

"Well, anyone who had killed one of us will bear its mark on the forehead all his life. You killed a 'were tiger' in your past life, and, as you still bear the memories of that life, the marks stay."

Mat Hijau reached out and stroked my forehead.

"See these creases between your eyebrows? That's the mark of a 'were tiger' killer."

"Marks—?" I was incredulous.

"Now what you are left with are the creases that spell 'Kating'. In our language, it means Killer of 'were tigers'. No wild animal, not even the wild elephant will dare cross you. No strong being will feel comfortable with you for long because you emit a form of energy that subdues them." He looked at me in silence for a moment before continuing.

"Those who are weak will not suffer the effects, whether animal or people—they in fact will benefit from your presence— but those who thought themselves strong will find your presence overpowering and will have to leave the room. Am I not right?"

I could find no answer to Mat Hijau's question, but wished his assessment true. There are thousands that need my subduing, I smiled to myself.

"What a nice aroma! Am I in time?" someone shouted from the forest path below.

Pak Samad! His form gradually emerged from the darkness. Still dressed in white with his black songkok cap and holding his umbrella.

"What are you cooking?" he inquired as he came near, full of smiles as usual.

"Deer, Pak!" I said.

He patted me on the shoulder and nodded to Mat Hijau.

"*Dapat?*—Did you get it?" he asked as he sat himself on the rung.

Hijau nodded, smiled and pointed at me.

"It's because of his presence, it came sooner than we expected. Two days only, it took!"

I realised they were talking about the Spirit of Cane.

"Show!" Pak Samad asked me. I took out the little piece of black wood from my pocket, no bigger than a sunflower seed.

He smiled.

"Good, now we have to put it in him."

"What? In me?"

"Yes, so it will stay with you forever. It must not touch the ground. Hijau did you not tell them that? Once it does, it will just disappear into thin air."

"Sit!" he ordered and lifted my shirt. "Hijau, will you prepare him please?"

Mat Hijau came closer to me, sniffed my back and before I could protest, started licking me with his tongue on the edge of my shoulder blade. First I felt the intense pain as his tongue, like that of a tiger's, was like a rasp grating the skin of my back, then the numbness set in. I could feel blood trickling down my back. Hijau held me firm as Pak Samad approached from behind with the Spirit of Cane. And with a push of his fingers, I felt something lodge under my scapula.

"Good. It is done. No one can extract this from your body, unless they know where to look and cut you up for it. But then, they can't cut you now."

The two men laughed.

"Don't worry, it will heal," Mat Hijau said, patting me on my back.

By then, it was time for our first decent meal. The three of us sat on the rung and ate our fill of the rendang. Mat Hijau lit up his puchok and offered us some, but we declined. Then Pak

Samad, after keeping silent for awhile, spoke.

"Mat, thank you for taking care of my student, Si Jan, and thank you a thousand times for giving him the Spirit of Cane. I will be taking him with me later tonight."

I was surprised at this announcement and sad at it too.

"Tonight?" I asked.

"Yes, it is time," he replied. "You have a lot to learn and so little time with us, Jepun!"

"I know he has to go," Mat Hijau nodded his assent while rolling another puchok. "He has been a great help."

"Oh, by the way, what did you do with your piece of Spirit of Cane?" Pak Samad asked. "Is it inside you too?"

"No, I let it go," he said.

"Pak Hijau, why did we go through all that trouble and you let it go?" I asked.

"Mat has his reasons," Pak Samad interposed.

"Why, Pak Mat?"

"Ah, I am old and I am tired," he answered. "Who wants to live forever?"

Chapter Seventeen

"This way." Pak Samad pointed towards a clump of trees as we walked down the path, away from Mat Hijau's pondok. I had been walking behind Pak Samad for most of the time deep in my own thoughts as to where I was being taken and why.

Parting with Mat Hijau was sad, even though I had known him and Rahim for only a short while. I had grown rather fond of the pair but I knew I would never see them again. Mat Hijau only patted me on the shoulder and smiled.

"You have very far to go, so be careful." And then he added almost as an afterthought, "—careful of Mankind."

Pak Samad seemed to have timed his arrival at the appropriate moment to take me away. I would not know what else I would learn from Pak Hijau that I perhaps shouldn't.

"Stand here," Pak Samad ordered. The night was dark, but appeared more 'velvety' at that particular spot. He raised his umbrella and stabbed the darkness, finding a slit in the dark fabric of the night, and moving it down, unzipping it further.

"*Mari, kita, masok!*—Come! We're going in!" he said, grabbing my hand and pulling me into another dimension.

I found myself in another world. There was no moon or star and no sound and no ground to stand on, and yet we were not floating.

"I am taking you into our Hari Kong; this is just the perimeter, the fence and the most confusing, where there is no Time," he said.

"Those who are not skilled enough and meddle with our Hidden Knowledge, those who dabble without a proper Master, may find a way in, but not a way out back to our world. So stick closely by me," Pak said leading me on.

I could see a lady, ancient in her features. I tugged at Pak Samad's hand.

"Who is that?"

"One of those trapped here for a long time."

"Why don't you set her free?" I asked.

"Well, she gained entry through evil means, so she has to stay here for a long while."

I had thought this Hari Kong place was just one of joy and pleasure and learning. How wrong I was. We went further in and met a younger man coming towards us. I recognised him immediately.

"Eh Halim!" I shouted as he came past. But he appeared not to have heard me at all.

"Pak Samad! That was a friend of mine," I said, "my childhood friend!"

"I know. He had been dabbling in the occult under a certain Si Amir, who claimed to be a powerful Guru in Perlis. But the sad fact is that Amir is a fake and could only teach Halim to a certain level, enough to enter our Hari Kong, but not enough to find his way home. Your friend will be here for only a short while, don't worry, this is just to teach him a lesson," Pak Samad said with a laugh. "We have to go, don't worry about him," he added, "I'll set him free on our return."

From the corner of my eye, I could see Halim trying to push at one point of the dark curtain and then another, each time failing to find the slit that would let him back to his world. One can see outside Hari Kong, the black curtain, when one is powerful enough. But when badly trained, one only sees the black curtains and nothing through them. I gripped Pak Samad's hand even more tightly.

I could only see the solid dark space as we moved.

"It won't be long," Pak told me.

A brightening lay ahead as though we were approaching a dawn of some kind. It became brighter as we moved ahead and I could see more. Not far from us, there appeared to be groups of men huddled together in conversation or debate, some gesticulating with their fingers and some with their hands, but all in a spirit of friendliness. Men and women of all colour in groups, some doing the talking while others just stood around and listened.

"Ah! Mrs. Newas! How are you?" Pak Samad spoke in Malay to an old Eurasian lady. White-haired and kind-looking, she answered while beaming at me.

"I am fine. Is this the young man you told me about?"

"Yes, our Jepun!" Pak said in reply. "He is my student now, I have brought him here to show him what Hari Kong is like."

"Have you told him what Hari Kong is for?" she inquired.

"Jepun, Si Jan, like I told you before on the jetty in Anson, Hari Kong is the space between Time itself—a place where we can escape to, to take refuge, to consult our superiors, to learn and even to reshape Time," Pak continued with my first lesson.

"Reshape Time?"

"Yes, Time can be moved back and forth. What happened yesterday can be altered and an event changed. Something in a particular place—say an apple on a table—may not be in that same place when we move Time back to before it was placed there by whoever."

"Or we can come out of Hari Kong and snatch that apple on the table," Mrs. Newas interrupted with a laugh.

"I am sure you have had experiences of things suddenly appearing again after being lost for a long time, in a place where you least expected to find them?"

"So would it be you and your kind that is responsible for things that disappear?" I asked.

They looked at each other and shook their heads.

"No, not always," Pak said. "Usually it would be because of your forgetfulness that you misplace things. But sometimes it can be the others from the next world being mischievious."

"The next world?" I asked.

"The next world is populated by the Spirits of those below. They were never born from a woman, and have never known life on our earth. From shadows they came, and in shadows they exist, and from shadows do their mischief and harm. They will take things they fancy, manipulate events just to see the Living suffer." Pak Samad looked around and waved to someone approaching whom he knew.

"They are just not nice," Mrs. Newas assured me in English. "Not nice things," she continued, wrinkling her nose.

"Ah! Samad! Is this your Jepun?" asked a huge frame of a man as he reached our little group. "Jepun! Still trying to find home?" he laughed, as he looked down at me.

"No more home, no more the old you. Soon you must let go of your present self too, Jepun, if you are to be a Mystic."

"Datok, he is still young, he will learn," Mrs. Newas came to my defence. "I will show him, slowly."

I felt sad at having to be reminded of all that I had to let go.

"Lose all, Si Jan, and gain all," she said as she slipped her plump hand into mine. As Pak Samad walked away from me in deep conversation with this Datok, Mrs. Newas took me aside to teach me more.

"Si Jan, don't take to heart what the Datok just said. He has a very direct manner of speaking, but he means well. He is the caretaker of this part of Hari Kong."

"Jepun, or shall I call you Si Jan? Look at the ordinary wind, has it form?"

"No," I said.

"Well," Mrs. Newas said, "it is all around everywhere it wants to be. What happens when it has form? Exactly, it can only go so far and no more. So it is in the case of a Mystic. To have no attachments, no possessions of material or personal worth or regard, one can fit into any thing or situation. Like the wind, one is free. Free to travel between places, situations, Time, Space or

Dimensions. Just like what you half learnt from your Fat Aunt, to materialise or disappear!" She smiled and patted me on the head.

"We made you stay with the 'were tigers' of Korinchi so that you helped them capture the Spirit of Cane. You could, but we couldn't," she added.

"But why not?" I asked.

"Well, none of us here have killed a 'were tiger' before. You did, in your past life, and yet you are able to stay above ground after your death in Burma. That is what has made you special—being 'in between' the two lifetimes."

So am I a blood-soaked Mystic?

"Who was I in Burma? Or, rather, who was I in Japan?"

"You will know when that time comes; you have a lot of this life to live. You will know soon enough when it is time for you to end this life," she said, without a smile.

"It won't be too long," she added.

Chapter Eighteen

I looked around at the others. There must have been at least fifty or more, in quiet conversation in groups of three or five.

"Do you notice anything about us?" Mrs. Newas asked.

"Well, I can see that you are all from different places of the world, judging by the colour. I can see whites, yellows, brown and blacks amongst you all," I said.

"Yes, but what else?"

"You are all very old."

"Precisely! Some may look young at a distance, but they have not aged since they came. You see, in this place, Time stands still. There are almost no real young Mystics at our level these days, almost none, Si Jan, or shall I call you Jepun? The world has changed. People value money and all that it can buy. The world has no time or need for Mystics, I mean the real ones. They won't even know if one lands on their head! There are so many poor imitations of 'Mystics' that are there solely for the money that their followers or believers will shower them with. They need to resort to cheating their followers and eventually themselves with their so called miracles."

Our conversation was interrupted by the arrival of a man panting as he ran past us. We could see that he was bleeding from a large gash in his abdomen.

"That's another use of Hari Kong," Mrs. Newas turned back to me to continue her talk. "Warriors or fighters who are able to access Hari Kong can slip in to repair themselves before setting out again to finish whatever they were in combat with. Don't worry about him, he will heal himself before you know it."

I watched this man, now seated on the ground, Buddha-style, as he massaged the wound with his bloody hand. The nine-inch gash then disappeared and even the blood on his hands somehow evaporated. He smiled as he got up and told the few who gathered around.

"Ah, that was close!"

"What happened?" asked another.

"They were out to kill this poor man, so I jumped and placed myself in between him and the mob. I allowed them to slash me with whatever they had. The screams of pain and my dying in front of them distracted their attention as they watched, thus allowing their victim time to flee the scene to safety."

The group listening broke into laughter.

"And you disappeared right in front of them?" asked another.

"Of course! I needed them to marvel at my disappearance and, so doing, soften their animosity towards that poor fellow."

"What had their intended victim done?"

"Nothing. He was an innocent man whom the mob accused of stealing. The guilty one was with the mob and he was the one who tried to kill this poor fellow and get off scot-free himself. So I allowed him and his friends to stab me instead."

"Right, I have to go back now and right the wrong," he added, now standing up and giving us all a smile as he ran back to where he emerged from.

"You see, Jepun, your Teacher Pak Samad will teach you how to access Hari Kong when the time comes. For the time being, you will have to stick by him when he leaves. We do not want you hanging around here doing nothing," Mrs. Newas said as she pointed me in the direction to where Pak Samad was standing, still in conversation with the Datok.

I shook her by the hand and bade her farewell.

"I'll be watching you!" She waved cheerily as I walked towards Pak Samad.

"Ah Jepun, I hope you are comfortable with Hari Kong. Your

Teacher will bring you home now. Come and join us when you are ready or when you are in trouble!" Datok laughed.

Pak Samad took my hand.

"Are you ready to go home?" he asked.

"I suppose so," I said. "What else can I do? He took me in here and I'd better not linger as I have no idea what I have to do even if I wanted to stay on."

"Do you not want to give him something to take home?" Datok asked Pak Samad.

"He has the Spirit of Cane in him, and for the time being, that should be enough. Other objects of power will find him in time," Pak Samad said and giving my hand a soft tug, led me away.

"Come, we must take you back, Hari Kong is a good place to be in when necessary and to travel from one place to another. But there are other ways, more enjoyable, ways of travel, as you will soon see."

We walked back towards the general direction whence we came, I presumed, as there were no landmarks that I could see— just a darkness where Time must have stood still for aeons on end.

"Your friend, Halim, I think we will let him out now," Pak Samad said. Even as we came closer, we could see him, oblivious of our presence and still trying to charge at the curtain of black, and being thrown back time and time again.

"*Ah, hutong belang ganishi yang belang, tinampanan adi rasa rasa sejati rasa,*" Pak chanted, and with his umbrella jabbed at the Darkness in front of my confused friend. There appeared a chink of light and then a slit in the black screen. I could see in the distance some limestone outcrops and some teak trees in the foreground.

Pak Samad gave my old friend Halim a push. He tumbled out, hands waving, trying his best to break the fall. Pak Samad laughed.

"He is in his Perlis now, only some ten miles from his house. A walk will do him good. This should teach him a lesson about dabbling in Mysticism. I hope he finds his so called Guru Amir and gives him a sound thrashing."

 But knowing Halim, I knew he wouldn't.

"He won't," I said.

"What do you think he is going to do?" Pak Samad inquired.

"That bum will team up with Amir and write a book and sell it to the stupid Americans to make more money!"

"*Nak buah buahan?*—Want some fruits?" Pak Samad asked, shaking his umbrella at me, still laughing.

Why not? Hari Kong might be timeless, but, boy, was I hungry!

Chapter Nineteen

P ak Samad just walked through the dark curtain, with me following close behind. We emerged into the bright sunshine, not far from the Tapah Road Station. The two of us walked beside the track, an old man dressed in white and wearing one black shoe on his right foot and a white one on the other, closely followed by me, a dishevelled youth with ruffled hair and mud-stained trousers and shoes. We must have looked a comical pair.

"Ah, Si Jan, we must get some money," Pak Samad said, stopping beside a nearby bush.

"Money? Where from, Pak?" I asked.

"Here," he said as he plucked at a few leaves from a wild cinnamon tree. "Red, ten dollars; green, five dollars. No need for the blue." He smiled as he stuffed them into his trouser pocket.

The Indian station master wasn't too happy to see me again,

and examined Pak Samad with some curiosity if not suspicion.

"Ah, two tickets, one for Tampin, please, and one straight to Singapore," Pak announced.

"*Ada duit tak?*—Have you the money?" asked the Indian fellow.

"*Ada, banyak oh!*—Yes, and plenty too," Pak Samad said pulling out a stash of banknotes from his pocket. A bundle of red ten dollar and green five dollar bills. They were just leaves before. Pak Samad looked at me and smiled. He counted the correct amount and handed them over to the still suspicious Indian station master, who then grudgingly clipped the two tickets and pushed them over the counter.

There was no one else waiting for the train, so the two of us just sat on the bench on the platform and enjoyed the sunset. Pak Samad reached into his folded umbrella and pulled out two curry puffs and two pears. "One each," he said. "They are quite juicy, these pears, straight from the fruit shop in Ipoh."

I could feel the cold on the fruit.

"It came from a fridge?"

"Yah, and the curry puffs came from Anson."

"How can you take them, just like that, without paying?" I asked, with some doubt as to whether I should eat something obtained illegally.

"No, they are not illegally got," he said, as though reading my thoughts. They are all paybacks. The shopkeeper in Ipoh had underpaid the pear dealer by telling him a lie, and the curry puff seller in Anson had overcharged his customer. We Mystics just make things even, we level the playing field."

"What about our tickets?" I whispered.

"Don't worry, we only travel in third class, and there are more than enough empty seats on the approaching train. We don't ask for much, just a little space in this world. Is that so hard to find? Just a little space, just a little space," he repeated and stood up. "The Indian will forget he ever saw us and will only wonder why he has so many leaves in his drawer the next day."

The train arrived from the North a few moments later. Three passengers got off and we got on. After a few minutes, a whistle sounded and the Indian station master waved us on. As our coach passed him, we could see his confused face when he saw us through the window. The whistle, dangling from his mouth and his hand clutching the green flag and waving it ever so gently as the train passed. I laughed at our little mischief. No guilt now, as Pak Samad explained, all we wanted was a little space, just a little space.

"Si Jan, I have just spotted a friend sitting in the next

compartment, so will you sit here and wait for me?" Pak Samad said after a few minutes.

The night was setting in, and the coach now dimly lit up by a few lights on the wall. I spent my time gazing at the little shacks or huts of the people who lived beside the track. Clusters of houses lit up by oil lamps and children still out playing games after their evening meal. Nothing had changed and the world seemed to be at peace.

Some three station stops later, four youths came in to 'our' compartment. I could sense that they were into some mischief or other, by their swagger and their turned up short sleeves that exposed their tattooed biceps.

"Little Chinese gangsters," I thought to myself. Tattoo of a dragon on one and the other three had various Chinese warrior Gods on their skin.

I looked away and ignored their posturing. Not too happy with my nonchalance, one walked over and banged on my table with his fist.

"*Apa? Lu Takut ka?*—What, you afraid?" he said.

I kept my cool and remained still, staring out at the window. A hand grabbed me by the collar and I was lifted up on my feet by that 'dragon boy' and violently pushed back on to my seat again. I sprang up and slapped him on the face.

"*Baka! Magai!*—Mad bastard," I said in Japanese, as my former self rose up in me. He staggered back, shocked by my retaliation. His three friends came at me together, each armed with a scout knife. The first man stabbed me in the abdomen. The knife hit a concrete wall. There was no blood, no wound and only a small hole in my shirt.

While I was marvelling at this sudden transformation of my body into one of concrete or even steel, I felt two jabs in my back, where the other two daggers tried to pierce. Again, the blades only hit steel. The two tried pushing their blades in, but without result, just making two tears on my shirt when their blades slipped.

Now in shock and probably more in terror, they stepped back but urged on by that 'dragon boy', they charged at me again with their knives aimed at my chest. Screaming profanities in Hokkein, the first two lunged, aiming straight for my heart. I stepped back and pulled them towards me by their wrists. Upsetting their balance, they went tumbling to the floor of the still moving train.

My mind was suddenly switched back to a snowy scene in Japan. I was on a polished floor of a training hall or Dojo. I could hear a Makiwara being kicked somewhere and hear its reverberation, of plank hitting plank and bodies dressed in white flying around, some hitting the floor with a bang!

Somewhere a voice shouted *"Sato–san! Sho-men–tsuki! Kote gaeshi!"* as the third thug lunged forward with his dagger, stepping over the bodies of his two friends and aiming his knife at my abdomen.

I floored this one too with that manoeuvre. Though the aisle was narrow, I managed to seize his wrist, twisting my body while still holding his wrist firm. I turned around to upset his balance and threw him, head over heels, on to his two moaning friends.

Now I was face to face with that 'dragon boy'. He smiled as he whipped out his switchblade, slashing left and right, then making straight for me. I caught the blade with my bare hand and, with a twist of my wrist, broke it. By then, I'd had enough of little gangsters, enough of light parlance with wrists or throws. As I moved towards 'dragon boy', I made sure that I stamped, hard on the three moaning men still recovering on the floor. I could hear a few bones breaking under my feet and the screams of pain as I moved on.

Our 'dragon boy' retreated and when I reached striking distance, I let out a yell that I have only heard myself do, a lifetime ago, a *'Kiyai'*, a shout to bolster or summon my internal strength as I released a punch on this fellow's chest.

His eyes bulged as he flew back and blood spurted as he collapsed on the floor. He just sat looking at me, speechless and panting.

I left all their daggers where they fell, beside the still writhing men. I stamped over them once again, just to have the pleasure of hearing a few more bones break, as I walked through the connecting door to the next carriage to look for Pak Samad.

At school, I was taught never to kick a man when he is down. They taught me that in English.

But I was—*I am Japanese and my name is Sato.*

Chapter Twenty

Pak Samad was busy talking to a lady dressed in black but with her face exposed to reveal that she was of some age. Her nose appeared pinched, almost beak-like, her lips just a slit on this wrinkled mask.

"Ah, Sato! Jepun! Come and join us!" Pak Samad cried.

Despite the noise of the train and the beating of my heart, I could not convince myself that he said anything else.

"What? You knew my Japanese name all along? Why didn't you tell me before? Why did you put me through all these," I said, jerking my head to indicate all that had happened in that last carriage. The old lady cackled and looked towards Pak Samad for his explanation.

"My dear Jepun, Mr. Sato," he said, giving me a slight bow, "there are things that you have to find out for yourself —no use if anyone of us tell you because you will never truly believe.

You need your past to tell you the truth, and what better way than that to give you back your name?"

"And what about those four that I have just hammered the hell out of—those four Chinese gangsters?" I said with some irritation.

"Well, you did them a favour, you saved their lives," Pak Samad replied.

"Saved their lives? How?"

"Well, they were meant to lose their lives tonight. They had planned to steal a car, but none of them could drive, so if they did succeed, they would have crashed and died. You, by giving them a beating, have prevented them from doing just that. They will suffer a bit, but they will change their ways and be better men in the future. So you see, we work in mysterious ways," Pak added.

The old lady cackled, rocking her frail self back and forth with her laughter. She kept her eyes almost closed as she glanced sideways at me. It made me feel uncomfortable as I stood by their seats.

"And besides, Jepun, you have tested the power of the Spirit of Cane. Are you convinced now that you are invulnerable?" he asked.

The train slowed down to a stop at the next station. The

door of the previous carriage opened and the four tumbled out. Our dragon boy first, pulling the other three out with some by-standers' help. We could see him gesticulating wildly at our coach and the small crowd that gathered turn towards our window. The whistle blew and the train started again on its journey South. A ticket inspector came into our carriage. *"Teket! tolong, teket!"* he asked everyone as he passed down the aisle.

Pak Samad looked at me and asked, "Shall we?"

I did not know what he meant, so I just nodded my consent. He said something to the lady, then took out his handkerchief and gave it a flick.

The Inspector passed us by as though we were invisible, and went into the next compartment.

"Pak Samad, what happened? What have you done?" I asked, incredulous. "Have you made us invisible? All three of us—invisible?"

"Yes, Si Jan, or Sato. I had to," he replied.

"But why?"

"Well, our train tickets would have disappeared by now, transformed into thin air just as the money we bought the tickets with have gone to become leaves again, so fair is fair. We wanted a little space on this train for you to have your little fight with those gangsters so that you would find out your name all by yourself, and also save those wretched lives. Now that it is done, we have little use for this journey anymore. We should leave now."

"But, Pak Samad, am I not supposed to be going home to Singapore?"

"No, not yet. Your exam results will not be out for another few weeks. We know you will be sent by your father overseas to study, so you will not have much time with us. Come, we must go," he said, now holding on to my hand.

"But Pak Samad, the train is still moving!"

The old crone cackled even louder and spoke for the first time to me.

"But we are not!" she said, pushing her face so close to mine that I could see the veins on her white eyes! She was blind! She gripped my other hand. I was too weak to resist. For this last hour, there had been enough shock and horror to last a lifetime. I just allowed them to take me towards a grey-coloured wind that blew across the breadth of the train and we 'floated' out as the train moved on.

Looking down while suspended in the silence of the warm tropical night, I could see the little dimly lit kampongs or villages of our people. I could see our train as it moved on, like a lighted millipede along its track below. We then changed direction and flew or floated towards a series of mountain ranges, their dark outline still visible against a starlit sky.

"*Gunong Ledang, tidak beberapa jauh lagi!*"—the legendary Mount Ledang or Mt. Ophir—the blind crone declared, "is not far away."

I had read of that famous place in our Sejarah Melayu or Malay Annals while in school, of Fairy Princesses, brave Warriors and other fabled Beings that inhabited the peak in times of yore.

I had also learnt that even the Greeks knew of this place and called our land the "Golden Chersonese", and now, I was being taken there by these two strange creatures, one who was supposed to be my Master, and an old lady who could only be a witch. And she looked a dangerous one.

The happy discovery of my name in my past life as Sato now paled with this new sensation of flight. I could feel the wind against my cheek and my body as we gradually descended from high and found a spot to land on the mountaintop.

"Jepun, this is another way of travelling, with more things to see," Pak Samad said.

"*Sini, Ikut!*"—Here, follow!—the old crone said as she hobbled on, leading us along. We followed her in the dark as she hurried down the slope, away from a man-built platform a few yards away."

"That platform was built by the Australian soldiers as their transmitting station," Pak Samad pointed with his umbrella.

Thank God, I thought to myself, at least we are on mortal ground and talking sense. No fairy platforms, but something real and man-made—by Australians, no less.

"So, who is this old lady?" I whispered.

"That's the Princess you read about in your history books, stupid," he said, walking ahead.

Chapter Twenty One

L ife is strange and those living are even stranger, in one way or another. There I was, just about to go home after those few eventful weeks in Malaya, and now I was being made to follow a blind crone, in the middle of the night, deeper into the Malayan jungle.

From what Pak said, if she was the Princess of our Legends, she would be almost six hundred years or more.

Courted by our Sultan Mahmud Shah from Malacca in the Fifteenth Century, she spurned his advances and fell in love with our own handsome Sir Galahad, one Laksamana Hang Tuah, the Admiral of the Fleet instead. He, as the Sultan's emissary, was sent to ask for her hand in marriage. But together, as legend would have it, they disappeared from this world. Hang Tuah, feeling the guilt of betrayal of the Sultan's trust, and she, just happy to disappear back into her Fairy Kingdom with Hang Tuah in tow.

All that I knew before setting foot on this fabled peak. Now to be told that this blind old lady, shuffling deeper into the undergrowth, lifting up one overhanging tree branch after another for us to pass through, was that Princess? What more awaited me? Was I being taken for another ride that no one would ever believe? Meeting a six-hundred year old Princess? This blind lady? Or was she blind at all? Before long, we reached a huge rock where she stopped.

"Wait, then follow," she said as she walked around it. Pak Samad held me back.

"Let me go behind it first," he said, "wait a few moments, count to ten, then you just come around too."

As he spoke, I could see smoke or fog flowing from the jungle floor, making a beeline for the base of this rock. What was more surprising was that the smoke was flowing under the rock, as though this megalith that towered a hundred feet or more, was actually suspended in mid-air. As I marvelled at the unfolding scene, Pak Samad gave my hand a pat to signal that I should be ready. With his umbrella, his pair of black and white shoes, his black songkok and his laugh, he walked around the stone and disappeared.

Left on my own, with my throbbing heart, I counted: One, two three—*but I really don't want to go*—four, five—*how am I to find my way home alone?*—six, seven, eight, nine, ten! I closed my eyes and walked round to the back of this ancient monument. I arrived straight into the middle of a celebration, and into bright sunshine. The darkness of the night was suddenly gone as soon as I rounded the corner.

Before me, was a riot of colour, of gold, silver, pinks and blue threads, woven into the ancient costumes of the women and men.

Pak Samad approached me, now wearing a Malay costume of gold thread woven on a black silk background, and wearing a traditional tajok, a folded silk head-dress, fit for a Prince over his now flowing hair. No more black and white shoes, instead slippers of woven gold on leather. But he wore the same smile.

"Jepun! Welcome!" he said, reaching out to me.

"Where is that old lady?" I enquired.

"Her Highness is with the ladies under that awning, she is being prepared to officiate at the wedding," Pak said. "She is the one seated on the throne and being attended to by the other ladies. See? They are fanning her now."

I could see no old lady, but a bunch of the fairest and prettiest maidens that I had ever laid my eyes on. And seated on one of the two thrones was one whom I would willingly trade my past thousand lives for. Her skin, the colour of light nutmeg and her hair, black and shining, and those eyes shone like the soft sunshine on the Sumida river. I was transfixed, as she turned to smile at me.

"That was your old lady, Jepun, the Princess herself," whispered Pak Samad.

I was speechless and just stared at the gay spectacle before me. Of men and women, well-dressed and busy with the coming wedding feast.

I could hear drums and gongs being beaten in the distance, and slowly approaching. There was this happy expectancy in the perfumed air amidst the laughter, music and the hand clapping.

Two well-dressed men approached me, and led me gently behind a screen of bamboo and silk. They urged me to change into something more suitable for the occasion.

"Now, wear these after your bath."

There was a large earthen jar of water beside us, and a small bucket with a long handle attached, floating on the water, a sort of a large ladle. That was our traditional way of bathing. One sits on the ground, scoops the water from the jar and pours it over oneself. But I was spared the effort. One of the men, invited me to squat on the ground, and did the honours. He scooped the water and poured it over me as I scrubbed myself pink with the dried husk of a coconut.

Something strange was happening. As much as the water splashed over my body and on the floor, this man's clothes remained unaffected. They were bone dry. He laughed at my confusion.

"It is alright, soon you will understand," he assured me.

After drying myself, I was given a set of clothes that would be the envy of any Malay Sultan. Sampin, a material woven on purple silk with threads of gold, to make up my long-sleeved shirt and trousers; they were a perfect fit. Over them, my sarong of black and gold thread, now tied by the men into a flowery knot, which was the fashion of the day.

"Your *tajok*, Si Jan," said one of them approaching me with my headgear held in both hands.

"Eh, this is only for a Prince," I said. "I am not a Prince."

"You are, Si Jan," he said, placing it on my head. A perfect fit. I felt regal, and strode out of the enclosure as someone with an official bearing. For once, I felt myself proud and confident. There were a few gasps from the ladies as they saw me. I was pleased.

"Now, here is a drink for you."

A young girl approached, bearing a cut green coconut on a tray of flowers. The cool juice was refreshing and the perfume that emerged from the tray of flowers was intoxicating. I was made to sit under an old Himalayan fig tree. Its large green canopy shielded me from the heat of the sun. Standing all around and behind me were men, all in a jovial mood. Sireh leaves were passed around, together with the pieces of betel nut and lime. Chewing like this is a pleasant, slightly soporific activity for natives in our part of the world; like the rolled puchok cigarettes, a social pastime.

"Where is the bride?" I asked one of the men.

"You will soon see her, Si Jan. It won't be too long. Be patient," he replied.

A procession of women came across the clearing, each laughing lady bearing a large metal platter of silver or gold, heaped with fruits and delicacies of all kind. I could make out our traditional Nasi Kunyit or turmeric rice, cakes made from glutinous rice, tapioca and even coconut. I felt ravenously hungry, but had to contain myself and observe the sense of occasion.

"The feasting only comes after the wedding ceremony," I told myself.

"Hang on, we know you are hungry," said one of the men, tapping on my shoulder, as though he could read my thoughts or perhaps spotted me licking my lips at the coming banquet

"Jepun, how do you find the ladies?" Pak Samad asked aloud.

"Beautiful! Absolutely beautiful!" I replied without hesitation.

In all these years of my life as Ah Jan, women had never been in my thoughts except one with a name called Kumiko. I could find no emotional attachment to any that I had met in this life, and had always stayed away, detached of feelings towards the opposite sex.

With my heart and mind still Japanese, I kept my distance and watched the fairer sex as any old Japanese man would— emotionally drained and devoid of any feeling that would involve the human heart. But, strange enough, all that changed when I turned around the corner of the megalith and into this world that I never knew existed. I felt my heart young again.

"Beautiful, Pak Samad—just beautiful! I have never seen such pretty women in my life." I hastened to tell him. He laughed and appeared pleased at my response.

"Wait till you see the bride," he replied as he walked back to the awning. His stride had changed. No more that of an old man shuffling along with his black rolled-up umbrella, he strode with the confidence of a Prince, much taller than I had ever seen him to be, and with the bearing of being Lord of all he surveyed.

I failed to understand how he could make this transformation in so short a time. I knew he could come and go as he liked, slipping from one world and into the next. I guessed he was that King Cobra whose tail I'd seized earlier, very probably, but to transform himself into a Prince? This old man with his umbrella, and with his black and white shoes? Well, that was the last thing I could think him capable of doing.

The drumming got louder. The kumpang players, our Malay hand drummers, used only on festive occasions, seemed to be approaching.

Krak! Krak! Krak! Kum-pung, kum-pung, kum-pung—kum-pung—krak tok krak tok krak tok—krak krak krak! The rhythm was catching as the drummers came towards our clearing.

Somewhere a trumpet sounded, and the nobat orchestra began to play. To a foreigner, the trumpeting can be likened to the sound of a bull elephant before a charge, the drums slow, deep and sombre. But those who know realise that these instruments are reserved only for the highest nobility of the land. Someone was being honoured.

The ladies that were seated on the ground at the feet of the Princess parted to reveal a young woman dressed in pink and silver thread, her headdress bedecked with strings of jasmine, and chempaka flowers. She looked shy with her eyes fixed on the ground, but, on her face, the faint trace of a smile.

"Is that the bride?" I asked the man beside me.

"Yes, isn't she pretty? Do you like her?" he asked me in return.

"That must be the most beautiful woman I've ever set my eyes on," I answered.

"Good, I am glad you think so," he smiled, patting me on the back.

A white-bearded old man, dressed in gray and silver, came forward, knelt down in front of our Princess and the bride-to-be, saluted them with both palms to his forehead. Then making a twist of his wrists, repeated the same motion again in their direction, three times. He spoke in a language that I had never heard before, which sounded like a cross between Batak and Khmer. After his speech, he saluted in the same manner and stepped backwards into the crowd, while still facing them.

The nobat drums played on together with the shrill pitch of a seruling or flute. Someone touched me on my shoulder, and the two men beside me helped me up.

"Si Jan, shall we go now? It is time to proceed."

With that, I was ushered towards the other onlookers at the circle.

There was a chair waiting for me, and as I sat, a man brought me a drink in an earthen cup.

"Drink this, you must," he insisted.

Overwhelmed by the friendliness and the hospitality shown

to me all this while, I dared not refuse. After all, I could smell a whiff of alcohol and perfume as I lifted the cup to my lips. Alcoholic nectar infused with the scent of a thousand jungle blooms was what entered my soul. I looked up to a throng of happy faces as they clapped and cheered. I had never felt happier in my entire life, what a people and what a paradise.

"Right, let the ceremony begin," Pak Samad's voice rose above the excited chatter.

I tried looking for him around me but failed. Glancing up above the crowd of men, I spotted my Pak Samad, dressed in all his finery taking a seat beside the Princess, who gave him her hand. Sitting side by side, they both smiled. Pak Samad even gave me a small nod and a wink, while the Princess looked on.

"Who exactly is Pak Samad?" I asked the man on my right. "Just who is he?" I asked again, my mind spinning uncontrollably.

"Who do you think he is?" he asked me in return.

Too shocked to answer, I asked him once more, "So, who is the lady marrying?"

"You!" came his reply.

Chapter Twenty Two

M e? Thoughts of my parents' permission, my former wife Kumiko in Japan, a job, a house and our future with children, flashed past my mind for almost half a second before I nodded my approval.

"Oh! Yes!" I gushed, forgetting that I was barely nineteen!

"Yes, you. Sri has agreed to take you as her husband," said Aweh, the man beside me. "I am to take you to her now," he added, helping me out of my chair and leading me to the centre of the circle.

The nobat drums began again as I stepped forth. There was an air of expectation amongst the crowd. I was made to kneel beside Sri, and together we raised our palms to our foreheads in salutation to the Laksamana and the Princess of Ledang. No longer was he the Pak Samad I knew, but—resplendent in his baju and tajok— he looked every inch the hero of our Malayan myths, our Hang Tuah of yore, the Admiral of Sultan Mahmud Shah's fleet.

Smiling from his dais, he leaned down and presented me with a keris, a Malayan dagger. It had a hilt of ivory, carved in the shape of a demam jawa—a shivering and feverish Javanese prince—the sheath, wrapped in gold.

"Since the two of you do not have your fathers here to present you with their kerises, take this, and accept that it is from your own father, Si Jan, and your father-in-law, as is the custom of our land. And this bracelet of black coral, the aka-bahar, will be a symbol that you are one of us to show the world. No one will dare harm you when they see you wearing it. Let it be your badge and wear it with pride."

"This"—with a signal to Aweh, who produced a spear from thin air—"this will be your hidden guardian, that will only appear when in dire need. Its name is Kriyat, remember it well. It will be in your hand only when necessary, otherwise it stays invisible, but will always be by your side."

The Princess smiled and leaned forward, whispered something to Sri and gave her a gold bracelet and a ring. The formalities appeared to have ended as the kompang drums took over from the nobat, and from the shade, a full gamelan orchestra started to play. Then the rebab [a stringed instrument], the drum and gongs started on a well-known melody. With the music, the dancing began with the men and women folk lined facing each other, swinging their arms to the music, their bodies close but never touching.

We were then invited to sit in rows with the others, men on my right side and the ladies on Sri's left. Fragrant turmeric rice, brought in large platters together with delicacies of all kinds, were then placed before us.

"*Sila bersantap*—Please eat and drink" Aweh said to us, using the language reserved for Kings.

Night soon came, and the merrymaking continued, unabated, but I could feel the weariness coming upon me as we had been sitting cross-legged all this while. I looked for the Laksamana and the Princess, and then at Aweh.

"*Beradu*," was his reply. Beradu, in Royal Malay, meant that the Royal personage had retired for the night. Who would blame two six-hundred year olds for an early night? Aweh smiled and asked me if we were tired too. Sri smiled and answered for me, by just a slight nod of her head.

We were led by Aweh and a lady-in-waiting, down a slope to a small hut, clean and smelling of freshly cut wood and fragrant jasmine.

"Your quarters for the night," Aweh said with a smile, adding, "you will be leaving us tomorrow at sunrise."

I was not sure if I should protest, as my idea of a union between a woman and man should be a while longer, as long as my old past tells me. But now, as a nineteen year old, I was as nervous as a cat thrown in water. I shivered and managed to mouth a soft 'thank you'.

Sri laughed and led me into the hut as the other two took their leave. The music of the night played on as she drew me down on a ready made bed of silk cushions. She touched me on my lips with her henna-stained fingers.

"Hush, we can only lie together for the night, and be man and wife only when you return."

"When I return?—when can I return?"

"When you have completed your task."

"What task?" I asked trying to sit up.

"Shh, you will know in the morning." She pulled me back, giving me a hug. "Don't worry, I will be here, waiting for you, or I will be with you anywhere, if you so wish."

As she drew her body closer to mine, I could feel it melting into my own, I felt her warmth entering me. The last time I felt that way was when I drank a whole bottle of Codeine cough mixture from Nosey's bedside, while he was dying of a cold and was fast asleep. Just like then, I felt consoled, warm and sleepy, and totally without a care in this world.

Who cares whether I had married a night heron called Sri Pelangi or a Peking duck for that matter.

What would the morning bring?

Chapter Twenty Three

Morning. I woke to the sound of a hornbill's flight. It sounded much like the creaking of an old door as its powerful but clumsy wings swept past our hut.

"You slept well," Sri said as she touched me on the shoulder. Her light brown eyes, still enchanting and her smile soul-consuming. Once again I could feel the warmth of her presence entering my being.

"Time to wake, Si Jan, and time to meet the Elders. Here drink some of this." She raised a cup to my lips. The cold liquid, sweet and fragrant, revived me. I felt young and ready to face what awaited me outside the door.

"Any food?" I asked.

"There will be, before you leave. Food is never hard to find here."

"Ah, sorry. How can I forget our Pak Samad or shall I say, the

Laksamana, with his black umbrella?" I said.

Sri just laughed. My old clothes, now washed and dried, lay beside the bed. I could see that they were serious about my having to leave. So be it. Life is short and parting is bitter sweet. Hadn't the Tokugawa haikus of Basho taught me that, so many years ago?

I was resigned to have once loved and lost, but was I in love with Sri at all? Was I sad, because of the memory of a Kumiko that I couldn't even remember or because I was leaving Sri behind?

There she was before me, one of the loveliest girls that I had ever set my eyes on. *But—do I love her? Dare I love her? How can I love her? She, who can transform herself into a heron and disappear into the night. Are they for real?* Sri read my thoughts, and embraced me as I changed back to my own clothes.

"You will be back with us before long, and we will end our days here. There will be enough time just to know and love each other. It doesn't matter if you love me now, or not. As long as I know that I do love a man like you and will wait till you can love and want me too," she whispered.

Heavy stuff. I had never held a lady so close in this lifetime. My mind was torn between the 'missions or tasks' laid out for me outside, or whether I should just shut the door and take her to bed, and this time no more 'airy fairy' stuff.

Sri laughed! "Don't worry, there will be time," as though she sensed what was on my mind. "We must go, they are waiting."

With that, we said goodbye to our little bamboo hut and walked hand in hand up the slope to the clearing above.

"Jepun, were you comfortable?" Hang Tuah asked, looking more like the Pak Samad that I knew. Still dressed as a warrior, but in a shirt and pants of striped brown cotton, with the sarong of woven gold folded short around his waist.

"Yes, Laksamana, we were and thank you," replied Sri on my behalf as she beckoned me to sit at his feet. Aweh, now dressed in the old fashioned garb of a Malay warrior, with his keris tucked in the fold of his sarong at his waist, patted me on my shoulder.

"Happy?"

"Yes, very happy," I replied and with no reason why I shouldn't be. There were some ten men around us, with Sri the only woman in the circle. They looked solemn. The joy of the previous day seemed to have evaporated and there was some serious business afoot. After a pause, Pak Samad spoke making sure that all could hear.

"We are happy to have you as one of us, Si Jan. I am sorry to have to appear to you as an old man to bring you here. There are things we can do, and there are things that we can't." He paused again and looked at all of us, and then back at me.

"Si Jan, look at this world, don't you see that there is difference in everything?"

I did not catch his meaning, so I shook my head and shrugged to express my ignorance.

"A tree is a tree, a chicken is a chicken and a duck a duck. The world of man is very much the same. There are blacks made black, whites made white, and yellows made yellow, and what have you. There are those who become Mystics for the right reasons and those who do for the wrong ones..."

I could see where he was heading and listened more closely.

"Now we have ducks trying to be chickens, and the world is now going upside down, with the farmer not knowing what to feed the chickens—chicken food or duck food."

The group laughed at his simple exposition. I suppose that was how things were explained in Malacca some six hundred years ago, so I laughed along with them. Ducks and chickens, what's next?

"Si Jan, Jepun! There is now an imbalance in our Mystic world. A Mystic's mission is to help put right what is wrong. He is the one who makes sure that the scales are balanced between Good and Bad, in order for Mankind to survive. He helps others in trouble through his Mystic powers with no gain or profit for himself.

"These days, the so-called Mystics are using their powers to help themselves for materialistic gains in the world of Man. So much so, that we are unable to maintain this Harmony. The world is now in turmoil as too many have pegged their lives on material gains by their practice of Mysticism of the worst kind. What they practice is the negative form of Mysticism, gaining powers through the use of violence on other creatures, including their own fellowmen."

"You mean Devil Worship and Witchcraft?" I asked.

"And more," Pak said. "By dealing with the evil forces and having truck with them, they have opened the door of the underworld. Evil has pervaded the world of men. We are now fighting a losing battle. Look around you when you re-enter your world. Evil men thrive and prosper while the honest and hardworking suffer. This delicate balance has been upset, hence the world—*your* world—is in turmoil.

"So what can we do?" I asked, hoping that I was part of the 'we'.

"We can't, but *you* can," he replied. "You, who came conscious from one lifetime and into this present one. You, whom we have endowed with some Mystic powers, can help us diminish these forces of evil and thus restore the balance."

"You see," he went on, "only a small imbalance is allowed between Good and Evil, for the world to be in a steady state, like a boat on the sea. We can only allow a slight shift from one side to the other, a bit to the Right then a bit to the Left, so that those living can see the difference between what is Good and what is Bad, and thus the world can be on an even keel. Just like serving you a good meal every time, then you wouldn't know what a bad meal was like, so you should savour some of both and so know the difference. What has happened is that this boat of humanity has tilted so far to the left that it may overturn altogether. We have to reduce these evil forces to the proper level for Mankind to have a relatively peaceful existence."

"Si Jan," he said, "we want you to go to a few places where these 'Fountains of Evil' are, try to extinguish them, and, in doing so, stop these so-called Mystics from doing more harm to the world.

Fountains of Evil. God! What next, I wondered.

"So where are these evil fountains?" I asked.

The Laksamana realised that I was being a bit flippant, and sneered before replying.

"In Bengal, in Nepal, in Tibet and elsewhere in the West. These are where the fountain heads are located, where their students of the Black Arts are trained. Disable them and give us a breathing space to regain the balance. Do you still have doubts? Look!" he pointed his finger at a brass bowl, filled to the brim with water. "Tell me what you see!"

"I can see the reflection of the sky, Pak. I can see the clouds," I said, still smiling. "But wait! Pak Samad, I can now see a room full of people! Yes, they are all around a man, dressed in black. Oh God! He is holding on to a child by her hair! A young girl! Oh God, I think she is about to be sacrificed! Oh God!" I looked at Pak Samad with terror. He wasn't smiling. He nodded his head and then patted me on my back.

"We let you see this scene, because we know that this Black Magician will not be successful as the authorities are on their way. Imagine how terrible it would be, however, if the Black Magician were to bring this ceremony to its grisly end!"

For once, I stopped smiling.

"Pak, how do we stop these things from happening?"

"You are to travel to these places, neutralise their powers and, if need be, destroy those Teachers and so scatter their followers. That should give us enough time and opportunity to restore the Harmony after a while."

"But you told me that there are only a few weeks before my exam results are due. How can I have the time?"

Sri and Aweh laughed, sensing that I was trying to wriggle my way out of this 'mission', this brave Japanese officer of World War Two.

"Do you not remember that we can stretch Time?"

"Jepun! How much time do you need? Two years? Two hundred years?" Pak Samad teased. "Your Chinese Fat Aunt has given you your Mau San powers, so has Mat Hijau, the were tiger. You have the Spirit of Cane, you have Kriyat and one of my kerises. What more do you need?"

"Nothing more," I replied, not knowing whether I had answered correctly. I had no idea what more I might need to defeat these evil forces, but then a battle is a battle. To fight one without blood and death is no battle at all, and furthermore I had resolved never to die again, anywhere.

"Where do I start?"

"You start in Bengal. You are to travel to Mymensingh, beside the Brahmaputra, then on to Pokra in Nepal and from there to Tibet, and then the West. Aweh will go with you, and so will Sri Kryiat, your spear. Others will take on those in North America, don't you worry," he added.

"When do I go?"

"After your meal. Didn't you say that you were hungry" Pak said, smiling at Sri.

Bengal! Where all the magic comes from, so I had heard in school a long time ago. And to Pokra? And Tibet where the Tibetan Lamas are? Who am I going to do battle with? But the promise of doing battle with my old enemies from the West, the British and the Americans, gave me a good reason to go on. How I wished I had my own Japanese sword with me.

"Si Jan, I will promise you this, when you finish these tasks, you will find your ancestor's sword, the one they killed you with," the Laksamana said, with some severity.

"No joke!" I shouted, forgetting that he was the hero in our history, the Admiral of the Sultan's fleet, albeit some five hundred years ago. Sri gave my back a pinch and Aweh a dark look of warning.

The cakes and biscuits served that morning were rather stale and soggy.

Chapter Twenty Four

Aweh reached up with his hand and drew down Kriyat from thin air.

"Here, Si Jan, see if you have command over Kriyat!" he said, handing me the spear.

The blade was thick and wavy, with the patination or Pamor called Buntel Mayit or 'Corpse wrapper'. It is not a safe Pamor or blade decoration to possess unless one is exceptionally strong in Mystic power, as it can turn on its owner and inflict untold harm and misery. It felt light in my hand; the shaft—made of ironwood, so dense that it normally sinks in water—felt to me as light as a broom handle.

"Go on; make it do things for you!" Aweh ordered as Pak Samad and Sri looked on.

"Si Kriyat! Go for that coconut tree!" I ordered as I flung the spear some twenty feet wide off the mark. But true to form, it went in an arc and embedded itself on the slim trunk.

"Wah! I've never seen such magic before!" I said loudly.

"Now, ask it to return to you!" Pak Samad ordered.

"Kriyat!" I shouted, stretching out my right hand "*Balek!*—Return!"

We could see it wrench itself from the tree trunk and head straight towards me, slowing down to settle on the palm of my hand.

"So how do I send it back?" I asked Aweh. He grabbed the spear and just threw it into the air. We could see it fly up to a certain point, then poof! It just vanished!

"That's how!" he said.

I bowed low to Pak Samad, our Laksamana and then to Sri and the others assembled.

"Jepun, take care. We will be here to guide you through these dangerous waters. Come home safe, come home to Sri. She will wait for you."

I bowed to them again and followed Aweh down the track to the floating megalith. I had the shivers when we walked around it and into the world of Men. It was already night and the full moon shone to reveal a carpet of mist still flowing towards and under the magic rock.

We walked for a mile or two until Aweh stopped at a clearing.

Around us was the jungle with its sounds of night birds, the howling of feral dogs at the moon, and the occasional crack of a rubber seed in the jaws of a wild boar.

"Aweh, are we going to walk to Bengal?" I asked in jest.

He laughed out loud and adjusted his sarong and his keris.

"Budak nakal atau bodoh?"—Young fellow, are you cheeky or just stupid?— then grabbing my arm, we walked into a patch of thicker darkness again. "We won't fly, but will travel through the Hari Kong, its faster!"

Moving in the Silence of Hari Kong, Space and Time was just like the folded paper of a Chinese fan. We travelled fast and far and reached our destination in less time than it takes to walk a mile.

Bengal had been in turmoil ever since the Indian Mutiny in 1857 that brought it into world attention. Home of the brightest men, of great thinkers, poets, writers and statesman, she has been mired in abject poverty and misery. Plagued by the twin sisters of natural disaster, flood and famine, Bengal had known few happy times.

"Could it be due to the practice of bad magic?" I asked Aweh.

"What do you think?" he said.

Aweh rarely gave a direct answer to a question. He would mostly pose a question in reply and you would probably answer the question yourself. Convoluted perhaps, but that is how the man worked. He was stout, muscular, and kept a moustache shaped like two downward-curving tusks, or commas. His nature was aloof and he had a far away look, as though waiting for someone or something to appear. He may have been of Bugis origin, those pirates from Sulawesi, most feared by the British sailors plying the tropical seas in the 19th century. The threat 'the Bogeyman will get yer', often used to frighten children to go to bed, came from their name.

We emerged from a bamboo grove by the banks of the Brahmaputra, into the bright sunshine of their summer. This slow-moving river originates from Tibet, where it is known as the Yarlung Tsangpo River, winds its way down Bengal to meet the Indian Ocean. Bengal is mostly flat, and so the speed of the river at that time of the year was sluggish and would be until the monsoons came.

"We camp by that sand bank," Aweh said, "at the water line."

Now hidden from view except by those on a boat sailing by, we set up camp and waited for the setting sun. We had not long to wait before the remains of the day was no more than a strip of orange on the horizon and the sky brought on a show of stars. On the far bank, a few fishermen's huts were lit up with oil lamps and no doubt the cooking-fires were busy.

"Hungry?" inquired Aweh.

"Not really," I replied, as the battle that lay ahead was still to be defined.

"It won't be long, just follow me and stay still, only move when I tell you to," Aweh ordered.

The night was turning cold and the wind moved the grasses beside us. Still we waited. Aweh had his hand on my shoulder; I could feel the pressure of his hand holding me down as though some danger were on the way.

Far away in the darkness, we could see a small flame approaching. No larger than an egg, it came towards us and sailed by, flying right above the water. Aweh drew out his keris.

"*Satiaksan!*" He shouted out, pointing at the passing flame. It exploded in a shower of sparks on the grey waters of the Brahmaputra.

More of these balls of flame came, from somewhere upriver.

"These are balls of Black Magic that our Mystic is throwing out to harm people his clients want him to kill. He does these things for money, this fellow; be prepared for more."

"*Satiaksan!*" he shouted as each of these flames came past, each exploding when it passed the tip of his keris, showering the river with red sparks. "Si Jan, now it's your turn."

From afar, a larger glow of red approached. We could see

it making a zig-zig zag motion on the river, as though it were on a search for something or someone. Aweh pushed me down behind the rocks as it passed, but its red glow revealed a black-faced Being, a woman with a long, red tongue, multi-armed, and carrying a large pot of flaming coal on her head. The noise of her passage sounded much like a train, a loud rumble at her approach, then the silence after her passing.

"She missed seeing us, I think," Aweh said standing up.

"Who or what was that?"

"That Being is the Black Magician's guardian spirit. She is the thing that gives him the power to do Evil, in exchange for the blood of animals and even children, which she feeds on," Aweh explained, sheathing his keris.

Just as he was doing it, the area behind him lit up. What just flew past us had returned. Aweh dived down, leaving me now face to face with this Demon. I could see her face, black and contorted. Her mouth red, framed by fangs at each side, and her tongue, long and dripping blood.

On her head was a pot of flaming coals and her numerous arms were moving like those of an overturned beetle.

I would have charged her with my Japanese sword if I'd had it with me, but alas, all I had of it was a vague memory. Left with no other choice, I raised my hand.

"Kriyat!"

The spear came as commanded, and I flung it towards the Demon. It hit home. The Demon appeared skewered, stayed unmoving, but dripping flames. Then it gradually settled on the ground, much like a deflating balloon. Spots of burning fat marked the place of her end.

"Sri Jan! We're going!" shouted Aweh, grabbing me by the arm as he ran. I followed taking Kriyat with me. Not far from our hiding place on the bank, we came towards a cluster of huts.

"Go around," Aweh said.

We skirted these flimsy reed and bamboo dwellings and came upon one all on its own. We could see some activity inside and a row of expensive cars and jeeps parked nearby.

"This is where he lives," Aweh said. Taking out his keris, he made a slit in the air, and pulled me in.

"Moving in Hari Kong, we can remain unseen until the right moment and emerge to do our job when the time comes. He may, if he is powerful enough, sense us, but it's quite unlikely as he would not have expected us to move in on him so soon," Aweh whispered.

We sat in the back of his hut, still undetected and watched this Mystic at work. He had already beheaded a goat and dripped its blood on this multi-armed statue to energise it to do his bidding.

The crowd of men and two women looked on, hoping to see something happen after so grisly a sacrifice.

"I need more blood!" the Magician announced, looking at his followers. "Our Deity needs more blood!"

He appeared flustered and unsure. His followers started looking at each other and then at a young whimpering boy tied up in a corner.

"Aweh!" I asked. "We move in?"

He nodded, whipping out his keris. We emerged back into this world. The Black Magician realised the situation he was in and aimed his dagger at my heart as I moved towards him. The blade only glanced away to my left. I could see the look of surprise and horror on his face as Kriyat plunged in. It all happened in a split second as we stepped back into Hari Kong. I am sure that all his followers ever saw was a blur of images from nowhere and the colour of bright red everywhere on the floor, just as their Guru requested, before they fled screaming.

'More blood!' Well, he got his wish, and so did we.

Chapter Twenty Five

We emerged out of Hari Kong sometime later at the upper reaches of the Brahmaputra and managed to wash the blood off Kriyat and ourselves.

"That, Si Jan, was just a skirmish, a training lesson for you. There will be more such encounters and more killings you have to do, on our behalf."

That I was a Mystic assassin did little to ruffle me. After all, weren't we all just State assassins as soldiers in any Army?

"A pity that you had to leave your keris behind with Sri," Aweh said, "but that I suppose is our Adat, our custom, and is necessary."

A man's personal keris represents him in all matters. So it was expected that it should be left to represent me in my absence from my wife Sri.

"You should acquire your own keris one day. On second

thoughts, why don't you let me make one for you?" Aweh offered. Before I could reply he stood up, clapped his hands together.

"*Baik lah*! Let me make a keris for you before I leave so that you will remember me always." How could one forget a man like Aweh?

"But where and when are you going?" I asked, feeling quite nervous of his reply.

"Don't worry, but leave you one day I must as I have other things to do too," he said, touching me on the shoulder as I sat there on the cool sandbank looking up to this warrior. There was a sparkle in his eyes now, like an excited ten-year old.

"Let's go! Let me make a keris for you while we still have time and in the process do a small favour for an old man."

"Favour? Old man? Where are we to go?"

"Islampur! Dacca!" was his reply.

Having no immediate need for Kriyat, I thanked it and sent it home in the way Aweh showed me. It just rose in the air when I threw it and then, as though taking a breath, it paused and disappeared.

Dawn was upon us—the river now a light pink and yellow reflecting the morning sun. The banks, planted with rape and now in bloom, laid out a feast of yellow against the blue of the sky.

How beautiful, I said to myself. Aweh heard me and smiled.

"I know, yet Mankind sees more beauty in the colour of money and blood."

"Shall we eat?" he asked, and, from the fold of his cotton tunic, he took out two freshly baked buns, then two mangoes, giving one to me. I couldn't stop myself laughing. First it was an umbrella job by Pak Samad or the Laksamana, and now this tunic job by Aweh. Could these guys not take along a shopping bag, even an empty one to perform their magic? I threw my head back and laughed out loud. Aweh laughed too, but asked me why.

"Kenapa?"

I just shook my head and laughed more at the idea of Pak Samad and this warrior with their shopping bags in tow.

"Nothing, nothing. I am just surprised, that's all."

He smiled, while stroking his moustache as he watched me doubling up in laughter.

"Shopping bags! *Pulak! huh!*" he said in perfect English.

"You speak English too?"

"No, I just read your mind," was his answer in Malay.

Now thinking back, they can all read minds! Pak Samad, Sri, and now Aweh! Thank God I did not think too badly of them. Still, no wonder the breakfast at our parting with Pak and Sri was served cold! A punishment of sorts I suppose, for being flippant and disrespectful.

From then on, I resolved to be more careful with my random thoughts and so be more open with Aweh or anyone else. It is better to be open and frank than to let others discover a hidden motive behind your words, especially when they can read minds!

"So Aweh, when do we leave?"

"Let's make some money first. Get me that pebble," he said, pointing to one beside my feet. I placed it on his right palm. He gently folded his hand, said a few words and when he opened it again, there was no pebble but a gold coin.

In my excitement I grabbed it to see if it was real. V.O.C., dated 1771. I had seen such a coin before in our National Museum. V.O.C. stands for the Dutch East India Company, which together with the British East India Company, was out here grabbing land for their respective Majesties. Now a payback I suppose for their plunder? And rightly so!

"Come, Si Jan, let's go, small adventure but good fun before we hit Nepal and Tibet. Let me make a proper keris for you," and with that we re-entered Hari Kong.

Chapter Twenty Six

Dacca was a riotous mix of colour and sound when we emerged from Hari Kong at the back of a bicycle shed. We walked out into the busy street, practically unnoticed except for three street urchins who followed us, pleading for baksheesh. A stern look from Aweh frightened them away.

"First, to that dishonest money changer, across the road from The Habib Bank," Aweh indicated.

The money changer was dark and rotund, dressed in white, with bulging eyes of a goldfish, ready to swallow up any unwary customer who walked in. Sitting behind a cage, with his radio blaring Bengali film music, he eyed us with some suspicion and then with pleasure when Aweh walked up to his counter and showed him the gold coin.

"*Koto Dam*?—How much?" he asked.

The money changer's fat palm reached out, took the coin,

looked, and fondled it between his fingers, then suddenly lunged at us, like an elephant seal.

"Where did you get this?" His eyes moved from side to side, almost in time with the drumming from his blasted radio.

"We picked it up from a beach," Aweh said.

"How much?" he asked again.

Our fat gent tapped something on his big calculator and held it up with a smile for us and the world to see—a paltry sum by any account. Aweh shook his head. Our man then retrieved his machine and tapped out another figure, doubling the first.

"Nah," said Aweh.

Back again, our giant tapped more vigorously and held the machine up higher and now glaring down at us sternly. Aweh acted agreeably and our man settled back on his seat with a humph! He then pushed a high stack of banknotes out the cage for Aweh. We left the shop and walked down the crowded street.

"You didn't count the money!" I said to Aweh.

"Why? All this for a pebble?" he said laughing as he hailed a bicycle rickshaw.

"Islampur!" Aweh shouted as we sat in. The old man strained as he worked the pedals.

"Why don't we just go into Hari Kong?" I asked.

"Nah, this is better, we just can't use the Hari Kong for our day-to-day business, stupid," Aweh replied.

We could see the seventy-year-old-looking man struggling on the pedals. Aweh laughed, said something and we sat, floating on a cushion of air with no weight on the seat. The rickshaw flew along; the driver, shocked to feel this sudden change and thinking that he had dropped his fare, looked back only to see us smiling.

It took him no time to join the mad jam of rickshaws as we headed into the narrow streets of old Dacca.

A place of ancient intrigue and murder, of dancing courtesans and fat Maharajahs lounging on fat pillows smoking opium or hashish in the days gone by. The word 'Dacoits' was supposed to have originated from the inhabitants of old Dacca, so I was told by Nosey not so long before.

We stopped outside a row of shacks and lean-tos. Aweh handed our rickshaw man a third of the banknotes.

"*Bhalo*—well done, good! Nah"—Aweh said.

The old man could hardly believe his luck and almost fell on his knees at this gesture from Aweh.

"Go!" Aweh commanded, and the old man, after tucking the precious cash in his sarong, pedalled away as fast as he could in case we changed our minds. Aweh smiled, shaking his head as he watched him go.

"All this for the money. Come, Si Jan, we'll visit an old friend," and he ushered me into the darkened doorway of a smithy. We heard a soft shuffle of clothes and something moved. An old woman, almost blind, looked up at us from the floor.

"*Motilal khotai?*—Where is Motilal?" asked Aweh. She lifted her gnarled finger and pointed in the direction of the room beside us.

"*Motilal aushook hoaychay*—Motilal has taken ill," she said.

We stepped past her gingerly and looked in the place where she indicated. On the bed, lay an old man who appeared to be sick for a long time.

"*Eh, Motilal! Aweh!*"

The man responded almost immediately on recognition of Aweh's name.

"Ah, ah Aweh!" he said, trying to raise himself from the bed. Aweh went over, held his hand and gently laid him back on the bed.

"*Kyamon ashen?*—How are you?" Aweh asked.

"*Bhalo!*—good!" which would be the standard reply even from a man at death's door. Aweh laughed, and placed his hand flat on Motilal's abdomen.

"Heart trouble, kidney trouble! Motilal!" Aweh diagnosed, shaking his head. He then moved his hand over the shivering man while mumbling a prayer. Motilal's pale greyish complexion changed. His eyes became livelier as Aweh chanted, then colour returned to his face and there was evidence of a smile. As Aweh droned on, Motilal was able to sit up wearing a surprised look and started to move his arms like a young nestling trying his wings for the first time. By the time Aweh had finished his chant, Motilal looked some ten years younger. He stood up, adjusted his lunghi and shouted for his wife.

"Eh Sashi Devi, asho!"

There was a happy reply from the room outside.

"Aaschii! Ami aaschii—Coming! I'm coming!" she answered.

A much younger version of that old lady outside the door stepped in, now well-dressed in a brighter sari, she smiled and bowed low.

"Aey amar Bodhu hoi, Si Jan—This is my friend, Si Jan," introducing me to the couple. It turned out that Motilal was both a silversmith and an occasional blacksmith. He was one of the best in Dacca until his sickness some two years before. Being a Hindu, he and his talents were confined to these slums of the city, and he could only work on commission from the Muslim jewellers.

Now restored to full health by Aweh, he was anxious to repay us this big favour. Aweh gave him the rest of the cash and told him to fetch some coal and the bits of iron he needed, and to start his little forge going.

"We'll make your keris here, in this little forge, Si Jan."

When the forge was finally lit, and with Motilal working the bellows, Aweh started on the few strips of iron, pounding and welding them together as he chanted. As night fell, Aweh finally deemed the red-hot piece of metal to be ready. Lit by an oil lamp, I could see the sweat and strain on Motilal's face; Aweh, with his mind on his work, kept pounding the flat piece of hot metal, chanting with each blow of the hammer.

"*Hong Rajah Besi . . . Semerliang Buku Bulu.. tekepong . .*" until he shaped it into the recognisable shape of a keris. That distinct feature of a snake-like blade, and the uneven lengths of the crossguard, longer on the right and less so on the left.

"Now for the last part," Aweh said, smiling at me while I watched in fascination as he handled the red-hot piece of metal with his bare hands.

Still chanting, he pinched along the blade and laughingly counted: "*Satu, Dua, Tiga . . .Empat, Lima, Enam. . . Tujoh!*—1, 2, 3,...4, 5, 6...7" Finished!—as he plunged the red hot metal into a nearby trough of water.

I was asked to lift the keris blade from the trough after it had cooled, and in the light of the lamp, I could see Aweh's fingerprints on the metal. Seven thumb and fingerprints on each side. In my hand was a Keris Pichit, one of the rarest, most sought-after blades from our region. Easily recognised by the presence of these fingerprints, which can only be made by a highly-evolved master smith who is impervious to fire and heat. Such blades are believed by all to possess great mystic powers.

"Si Jan, here, this keris is for you," Aweh said. "Keep it well, guard it as it will guard you. Its name is Kyai Aweng, remember it well as you will remember me." With his outstretched hand, he snatched a silver sheath from the thin air and his friend Motilal brought forth a well-decorated silver handle. Now with my keris properly assembled, I felt like a grown man, and whole once again.

Aweh studied the keris for another time, showing me the Pamor Adeg, the surface decoration being a stream of unbroken lines of folded metal, much like the skein of a girl's hair. He handed me back Kyai Aweng and appeared satisfied with his work. Dawn would soon break as the sky was becoming brighter. Smoke from the cooking fires had already begun to rise and somewhere a cock crowed his majesty.

"We go?" Aweh asked me.

"I think so, and thank you, Aweh, for the keris," I said in

reply.

"That's nothing. You will have to learn to do all you just saw and more, before I leave you."

Now with his hand on my arm, with his own keris he made a slit in the air and we went away from Motilal, Islampur and old Dacca.

"Aweh, you reversed Time for Motilal, didn't you?" I asked.

What do you think?" was his reply.

Chapter Twenty Seven

Now safely back into Hari Kong, this day between days for the Mystics, we settled ourselves in its Silence. Two souls floating in a darkness of nothing.

"Si Jan, you will have to learn all that you have seen us do so far, because what lies ahead will require you to pull your own weight, whether I am with you or not," Aweh said, without looking at me.

"How do I learn all those chants and magic manoeuvres in so short a time? All those things that I saw you and the Laksamana do?"

"Si Jan, Time can be stretched, or even reversed. What is important is whether you have the ability to absorb all that I will transmit to you," Aweh replied. "If your cup is full to the brim, like most men, full of nonsense and trivia, there will not be space for you to absorb what we have to give you. So the first thing is to clear your Mind of all thoughts and only listen to my voice, with no interruptions in your concentration. That is how you learn."

"So when shall we start?"

"Now?"

Aweh motioned me to 'sit' and concentrate on the unmoving flame of a candle in my mind. I should see only an unwavering light, and when I felt ready, I was to give him a nod. It did not take me long to do so.

"This is the charm for Halimunan, or Invisibility," he said as he went on intoning the magic verses, then shortening them all into one word for its immediate effect. Just like telling you to 'run into the house as there is a mad dog on the loose', but, now, just using one finger to point towards the door and say 'run!' for the same effect.

"The Laksamana told us of finding you at the Tapah Road station, coughing blood. That would be because your training was not complete before you attempted this disappearing business. So the next time, do it the way that I have just taught you."

Next was the Art of Transformation.

"Everything will work, it just depends on the power of the Mind. The stronger one is, the more successful one becomes in any undertaking. To transform yourself into someone or something else, it depends on how strongly you can hold on to that picture of the new you—be it a tiger, a snake or another man. Once you waver in your thoughts, that power is lost and it will be some time before you can rebuild the strength to do it again, so please take care!

"To return to your former self, you must first have a real, I mean *real* idea of what you actually look like so that you can fix your Mind on it and thus change back to your very own image." Aweh gave great emphasis to the word 'real'. "Many a weak practitioner will fail at this juncture, mainly because they do not have a real idea of what they actually looked like before. So they fail to be themselves when they return. Most become madmen or madwomen, and die miserably. So beware!"

After that lengthy instruction, he intoned the verses that I would need to absorb in my Being and then gave me the shortcut way of just using one of the words in that charm and the Mudra or finger sign to render its potency.

"It is not too difficult—or is it, Si Jan?"

"No, Aweh, not at all."

I felt a wave of gratitude sweep over me as Aweh imparted these teachings so selflessly.

"Now watch carefully, and see what I can change into,"

Aweh ordered.

First I could see him floating in the darkness of Hari Kong, then as I watched, his body turned a bit hazy, almost smoky. His smiling face remained the same, but his long hair and the headband gradually dissolved. On his head was the long yellow hat of a Gelugpa Lama, and then almost immediately, the yellow robes of a Tibetan monk were on him. The Lama smiled.

"Si Jan, will you do the same?"

I cleared my Mind of all thoughts, and fixed it on an image of another Lama I had seen in a book, *Seven years in Tibet*, not so long before. Then directing all attention on that image, I intoned the few verses, locked my fingers into the sign of a Mudra and, keeping my Mind fixed on that image of the Lama, said aloud the sacred word. I came away with a shaven head, a yellow curved hat, a thick string of beads in my hand and dressed in a swathe of dull yellow.

"Not bad! Not bad for a first time," Aweh said smiling. "But next time, don't shout the sacred word"—he patted me on the back—"just whisper it, alright?"

"Time to go?"

"Where to now, Aweh?"

"Where do you think?"

"Nepal?"

He nodded and pulled me through another dark curtain.

Chapter Twenty Eight

"We will be going into Nepal soon," Aweh said. "Change your keris into a kukri, we can't wear a keris there."

"Change my keris into a kukri? How?"

Aweh laughed, taking out his own keris and stroking it. The weapon assumed a thicker, darker shape, and slowly bent to become something of a boomerang, but with a handle at one end.

"That's how." He unsheathed the weapon and showed it to me. No more the damascened metal of a keris, but the shiny cutting blade of a Gurkha's kukri.

"How many waves has Kyai Aweng?" he asked.

"Seven," I replied. "You made it seven, wavy like a snake in motion."

"Good, take out Kyai Aweng, I think it has gone straight now."

Just like he said, the keris now had a straight blade.

"How can that be, Aweh? It had a wavy blade when we last saw it?"

Aweh laughed.

"Our weapons possess the power of change too, they behave just like us. They can take on different forms or shapes as ordered and they can come and go into Hari Kong as required. Remember Kriyat?"

I should have known, for wasn't that spear another of our weapons?

"So how do I turn it into a kukri?"

"Just stroke it and command it, and it will be," was his reply.

So Kyai Aweng gradually turned from a keris in a silver sheath into a kukri in a black leather one, topped with an ordinary wooden handle, as I willed it to be. Now it was our turn to be a pair of Nepalese. It wasn't too difficult this time as we had Nepalese traders selling their beads and bangles on the sidewalks back home.

Aweh gave me the last two teachings before we continued on our mission: the power of flight, and the ability to enter and leave Hari Kong. This last lesson was the most important of all.

"Si Jan, look around you. We are still in Hari Kong, in darkness. But look again, it is not uniformly dark. As everything in this world has different shades of existence.

"Some parts are darker, thicker and some only shadows of black and grey. Just like the world outside us. There are places even in daytime, which are brighter and warmer than others, whether there is shade or no shade. In everything, there exist different levels of Being, whether you can see them or not. When you look at the dark in Hari Kong, don't you see those darker curtains?" he asked. "Try. Look harder and show me."

I strained to see them, but he stopped me.

"That's where you fail, Si Jan. The straining makes you want to see, with your heart. That won't work. Relax and let your Mind's eye see, just do that, relax, then see what's in front of us."

I did just that and slowly I could see that there were—even in the darkness—billowing curtains of black that were blacker than the surrounds. I pointed them out to Aweh.

"Good, that's where you can cut a slit and come out of Hari Kong."

"So how do I get in, from the outside?"

"Do the reverse if it is daytime. Let your Mind see the thin strips of brighter light in the day. Cut through that and you will be back here in Hari Kong, in the darker than dark, so no one can see you. Of course, you will have to say these sacred words before you do, not out loud, but in your heart."

He then brought me closer and whispered the words in my ear. I had heard Pak Samad use the same verses before when he first took me out of Hari Kong.

"Now Si Jan, take us out of Hari Kong."

I took out Kyai Aweng, which had become a kukri, slashed at the dark curtain and we emerged in a clearing beside the Irrawaddy, somewhere in Burma!

"Wrong curtain! Si Jan! Ha! Ha! Wrong curtain, wrong turn!"

I laughed too, pleased with my first exit from Hari Kong on my own, though I should have faced North when leaving Dacca.

"Now we will go by the Mystic Wind instead, we'll fly," Aweh decided.

It wasn't too hard to fly, as we did it using the Mind and the power of the Mystic Wind. It was a case of just catching a ride on it as it came past.

I was with Pak Samad and the Princess on the train when we flew out into the night by grabbing a ride on that same Grey Wind. "These Grey Winds," Aweh explained, "blow criss-crossing the world, transporting thoughts and news as they go, to those who are able to harness them. You can send your thoughts to others, or messages on the Grey Winds too. It is also a convenient way for those in the mystic way to hitch a ride, provided one is powerful enough to spot one passing and then ride it."

"The only dangerous part in this exercise is that it is available to each and every powerful Mystic, whether good or bad! There are occasions where battling with an enemy up high can cause weapons, and even blood and limbs, to fall out of the sky. People on earth believe these artifacts have great powers, whereas they are just weapons of the defeated and so are totally useless." Aweh smiled, stroking his moustache while looking around.

It didn't take long before the two of us spotted the Grey Wind blowing across the dry field of rice paddy. As it came near, we grabbed it as it moved past and we soared up high. Not long after we could see below us the lights on the land. I noticed streaks of light rising towards the sky, much like searchlights.

"Aweh! What are these things?"

"The bright greenish ones show us where the good deeds are being performed on Earth and those dark beams on that side— that's where we will find the black Mystics at work, and those are the places we need to go to do battle. No, not just us—there are many of us with the same task: to defeat these evil ones so that the world can be brought back to some kind of Order. We can never defeat them all, nor do we want to, only the most evil ones. They must be cut down. Are you ready?"

"Yes, quite ready," I said. "We go down now?"

"*Anyah baling katimu!*" Aweh shouted, and we were dropped off gently on the ground as the Grey Wind slowed and then moved on.

"We become Nepali?"

"About time," Aweh said as he became less solid and gradually hazy.

I focused my Mind on a Nepali street trader I knew in Singapore as I followed Aweh in our transformation.

"*Kosto cher?*—How are you?" I asked him.

"*Ramro! Dhonabad! Timi Nepali basha tarcher*?—Good, thanks! Do you speak Nepali?"

"*Kina tarcher nah*?—If you can speak it, why not I?"

Two handsome Nepali traders were observed strolling into town, nothing special.

Just us.

Chapter Twenty Nine

The walk through the village track took us up the Khumbu Valley towards Namchee Bazaar in North Eastern Nepal. Surrounded by high mountains, it would be the last trading post before one climbs Mount Everest itself.

"Are we going to the top?" I asked Aweh.

"No, we turn off just before the village and down that slope towards the Dudh Kosi River. We are not here to plant more flags on Everest, Si Jan. We are here to pay a visit to that Bon Po magician down below."

"There are many so-called Mystics in India and Nepal. They are just there to extract money from those simple-minded followers from the Western world. These so-called Mystics are harmless, as they are without powers of any kind except that of deceit. We leave those alone, let the blind fool the blind."

A dark shadow seemed to cross his face as he looked at me,

and he paused for a moment before continuing.

"We are after that very evil Black Magician, a Black Hat Bon Po who uses the blood of humans, mostly children, to gather powers to do Evil. He has been doing it for many years and has reached a point where we have difficulty in eliminating him. You are to do it for us, Si Jan."

As we descended the slope towards the valley floor, we could see a small temple of sorts, with prayer flags fluttering in the wind. The place looked deserted. On guard was a Tibetan mastiff, brown with a black mane. It eyed us with suspicion as we approached, then without warning charged, baring its fangs and making a beeline for me.

A kukri is useless when the enemy approaches in a straight line towards you at speed and at waist level, unless you have time to turn and hack at his neck, beheading him in the process. As it all happened so fast, there was no time to use the kukri, but enough time for me to kneel on one leg, facing his charge and thrusting my hand into his open jaws and push till I could push no more. I then made a fist in his throat and held on. The dog tried to shake me off with his massive head and frame, but I held firm choking it and within minutes, it slumped to the ground dying without a whimper.

"I've never seen anyone do that before. You must not be

afraid to die, Jepun!" Aweh said, helping me up.

"What do you expect? Me, a former officer of the Imperial Japanese Army? Don't mess with me!" We both laughed as I cleaned the slime from my hand.

"By the way, Aweh, how can I ever die?

Before these words could leave me, there was a tremendous clap of thunder and an enormous Being, some fifty feet tall, stood in front of us, dressed in old Tibetan armour of steel plates laced with leather. It wore a ferocious mask, and carried what looked like a spiked mace. It looked at the dead dog on the ground then made a swipe at me with his weapon.

I managed to take a step back, the mace missing me by a hair. I could feel the warm wind as it passed my face.

"Kriyat!!" I yelled and the spear came, and just in time. I flung it at the Demon and it struck home, piercing it in the chest. As I took hold of the shaft and tried to push the blade further in, Aweh managed to run up my back and on to Kriyat's shaft, gaining height he reached the Demon's neck. With his kukri, he managed to cut into its neck before falling back on the ground.

The Demon, now mortally wounded, came back at us swinging his mace and emitting a ferocious growl as it approached.

"Si Jan, take over!" Aweh turned his back on me and with his kukri, made a slash in the air and disappeared, leaving me alone with this thing. Despite being abandoned, I was not going to run. Demon or no demon, we were trained never to surrender, that was our old army code of Bushido. I have often asked myself how much further a fallen cherry blossom could fall?

I wrenched Kriyat out of its body and aimed for its heart. But it was like piercing a hollow drum. This Demon thing was hollow! I managed to pull out Kriyat and took a step back to make another attempt, but I was too late. The Demon's mace smashed into me and as it passed through my body, I let out a cough. No blood, no guts of mine flying.

I was surprised as anyone would be. What was this thing that I was fighting?

I turned away and gathering Kriyat, made my own entry into Hari Kong. Aweh was there doubled up with laughter.

"Si Jan, I realised it was just the Black Magician's illusion, when I slashed at its neck and found it hollow. It was to frighten us away, that was all. So I came back here to take a rest and watch you fight with that 'thing'.

"So where is that very evil and very powerful Black Magician we are supposed to kill?" I asked.

"Here!" a voice in the dark replied.

Chapter Thirty

There was no time to be shocked or surprised or even to look at Aweh for an explanation. She wore a black hat, almost the size of a Mexican sombrero, with the long tail feathers of the Reeves pheasant stuck on. On her neck she had this thick string of turquoise and Himalayan coral, interspersed with the black claws of a bear.

On one hand, she wielded a long whip of banded human hair and on the other a brass bell. She looked at us with the shiny eyes of a madwoman, and her maniacal laughter confirmed that she was one.

"Mrs. Newas!" I cried.

She wasted no time with pleasantries as her whip caught Aweh unawares. It twirled around him with the speed of lightning, wrapping him so tightly that he could do nothing but look at me. With her other hand, she rang her hand bell and as she did so, some ten black figures emerged from her voluminous dress and ran towards Aweh.

I was at a loss as to what to do. This was a kindly old woman, whom we'd met not so long ago in Hari Kong, and now this 'thing' was out to kill us both? There was no time to waste as I could see her underlings tear at Aweh who appeared helpless to retaliate except to use his legs to try kicking them away.

A kukri or even a keris is only useful for close combat; it would be useless on braided human hair. Just then I remembered what Aweh told me about the ability of Kyai Aweng to change when ordered.

"*Kyai Aweng! Pedang Jepun!*"—Japanese sword!" and in a flash my hand held a trusty Japanese katana and even in the darkness of Hari Kong I could see its triple peak hamon or tempered line. The sanbonsugi of a Kanemoto blade, one of the sharpest! My confidence now boosted no end, I slashed and the sword, true to its fame, sliced through the whip, like a knife through a cucumber. I then turned to face the witch, while Aweh, now freed, battled against the little black figures.

She retreated a few steps and from her sleeves drew out a shiny sharpened disc, which she threw at me. The Kanemoto flashed, halving it. She threw more as she stepped back further, each time, my sword did my bidding, slicing each disc in two. All the while, I was judging the distance between us and when I saw it was right, I called for Kriyat. With the Kanemoto sword in my left hand, I threw Kriyat towards the fleeing Mrs. Newas.

She turned to run, using her black hat as a shield as Kriyat came, but she did not see or expect me to run with the spear as it flew. For a moment, I saw her smile, as Kriyat embedded itself into her hat.

I doubt if she even had time to look up to see me as I slashed down at her left shoulder, the blade only leaving her body at her right hip.

I was pleased with this tameshigiri or blade test. It was truly a good blade and that would be the second most difficult cut in sword testing. I felt no remorse, no guilt and no pity in what was left of my soul. Aweh came by to inspect my work.

"That's one real cut," he said. "You must have been really angry?"

"Nah, I just wanted to see if this is a real Kanemoto blade," I replied.

"No wonder we had been unsuccessful at eliminating this Black Hat. She, or it, had been with us all this while! She knew of all our plans against her before we set out, and so was able to escape us each time."

"Aweh, I thought that Hari Kong is only reserved for the good guys?"

"It is, she was probably good before, gained entry into Hari

Kong, turned evil and stayed," he said. "That must be how. Well, whatever. Evil amongst the Good will never have a good end," he said as he walked away.

"Where to now? Aweh?" I called after him.

"Where to? I am weary. Will you go to Tibet yourself?"

"Whereabouts in Tibet?"

"Let the dark lights show you," he said, fading away.

That was the last I saw or heard from my friend, Teacher and companion. He appeared downcast or ashamed for not detecting that Mrs. Newas was no more than a Black Magician in disguise, or maybe he felt, for once, defenceless in this last encounter. I do not really know why and, over the years, I have often pondered on the real reason for his leaving.

Whatever, now left alone, I decided to fly to some mountain peak and look down on this whole creation of Fairies, Angels, Demons and Man.

An Angel may be only a dream and a Demon just hot air.

Chapter Thirty One

Left alone in Hari Kong, I took my time as I drifted on. For how long, I know not. Maybe a day or a year, but who cares? Time stands still in the Silence of Darkness, there was no reason to hurry as the world would stay the same when I re-entered it, whenever.

I made sure I met no one, for I realised that I didn't really need anyone anymore. No more Masters, friends or companions. No more joys or sorrows, or sadness of the betrayal and of saying goodbyes. I would do what I had promised the Laksamana or Pak Samad I would do; then I would find my old self before deciding on a road for my new life.

I came out of Hari Kong not far from the village of Namchee Bazaar, it was night-time so it was easy to spot the Grey Winds as they blow up the slopes of the Himalayas; Tibet would be just over the other side of the mountain range.

As I flew over, I could see a whole rank of lesser peaks lined up after Everest, as though they were waiting their turn to be King.

Bright beams of light were shooting up to the sky everywhere, from their temple complexes to even the smallest hovels, but as I flew further on, and to my left, heading West, I could see a few dark beams doing the same. These were the places where Evil was being generated, but there were so many of them! Which one should I pick to battle?

I hovered around and watched. Down on my left, I could see a dark beam moving towards a bright green beam, almost attempting to overshadow it. Well, that is where I should go, I told myself, as I prepared for a landing nearby. "*Anyah baling katimu!*" I shouted as the Grey Wind paused in its path allowing me time to get off. I made myself invisible almost immediately as there was no need to reveal my presence so soon. I had landed in a courtyard of a small temple where that dark beam rose to the sky. I passed by a few sleepy, flea-bitten dogs and into the Inner Sanctum itself.

There were a few Tibetan monks surrounding an Indian Sadhu or 'Holy Man'. Unlike the well-wrapped Tibetans, this ash-smeared fellow was naked to his toenails save for a loin cloth. He had red lips and his eyes were bloodshot, his hair all matted and tied up in a bundle, all powdered with ash that made him a fearful sight to behold.

He was busy explaining to those around what he wanted to do to his enemy, not too far away. Taking out his short staff, made of a broken human thighbone sharpened to a point at one end, he started waving it around and chanting his mantras to invoke the help of various Evil Beings in his coterie.

The Tibetan monks could only watch in fascination. I could see that they were a bunch of frightened young novices. There was no sign of a senior monk, so I surmised that the old monk, their Master, must have died and these novices had been left to fend for themselves.

The 'Holy Man' had made a figure of flour, which he had laid out on the floor. In the light of the candles and oil lamps around the group, I could make out that this was the effigy of his enemy or rival whom he wanted to kill. Sensing my presence, he looked in my direction. Although I was invisible using the art of halimunan, anyone powerful enough could still feel that there was 'something' unseen in the room. With my keris, I made a slit in the air, and moved into Hari Kong and waited.

It must take a lifetime to kill someone that way, I thought to myself as each time I looked, he was still chanting, his voice rising as he screamed his curses at the little figure of flour. At long last, now drunk with his own power and importance, the 'Holy Man' stood up, raised his sharpened stake high up in the air, ready for that final stab into the little doll of flour.

That was my cue to go into action. In a split second, I came out of Hari Kong in the middle of the group, and lay on top of their effigy. The transformation from a lump of flour to a real man happened so fast that the monks could only spring back in total horror. I could see it on the face of the 'Holy Man' too, but now, thinking that he had actually materialised his enemy out of powder, smiled at his newly found power, as he plunged his staff into my heart.

It met steel as it scraped off my chest to hit the floor, breaking its tip. He jumped back, his bloodshot eyes now wide open, a face of utter terror as I stood up smiling and walked towards him. He had a dagger hidden in his begging bowl, an evil-looking weapon—bloodstained from the numerous sacrifices he must have performed on his way here. The killing of countless innocent beings in his quest for power.

With that in his hand, and looking like a being from hell, he screamed as he charged at me. I stood my ground, with my mind fixed on the image of a tiger, changed into one and roared. He dropped his begging bowl, the dagger and fell to his knees.

I am not here to love, to forgive and forget, I told myself. I am here to eliminate scoundrels like you! With that, I, as a tiger, tore into him mercilessly. With that done—messy it may have been—I became myself again in front of the seven trembling monks.

"*Tashi Daleg*!—Greetings!" I said in Tibetan. "Now bury him," I added. and walked out of their temple ready to go on my next mission.

Dough effigies! Hah! What was next? And what a waste of bread!

Chapter Thirty Two

A Grey Wind almost ripped into me as I came out of the temple, suggesting an element of urgency to carry me from my present situation. Latching on, I climbed up higher as it swept towards the western peaks of the Himalayas to Afghanistan and the West. The snow-covered mountain ranges came up to meet us as we flew over K2, the world's second highest peak, and on to Kabul, then to Mazaar e Sharif as we went.

There were very few green lights shooting up towards the sky, and certainly fewer dark lights that I could see. I climbed higher to reach the top of this Wind, and as I did, in the rarefied air, I felt that there was a message for me. Stifling all other thoughts, I listened carefully and caught the voice of Pak Samad. "Go to the British! Si Jan, go to Britain! But beware—danger is approaching."

My Grey Wind slackened as we passed another coming the

opposite way. I could see a few figures riding it. They were all armed and appeared hostile as we drew near. I could make out one, probably their leader waving his arm urging his fellow riders to jump on to my side. As we passed, all four of them clung to the lower reaches of 'my' Wind and climbed like apes upwards to me.

"*Pedang Jepun!*" I yelled at Kyai Aweng, as I drew the keris, and in a flash, I was gripping the handle of the Kanemoto. I then pushed myself off the wind and, as I fell, met in turn each of the four riders in combat. The topmost one was the leader, a wizened-looking man who wielded what looked like a Yataghan, a sword from the Caucasus with that downward curving blade.

He slashed out at me as I dropped past, but I was faster as I was holding on to nothing except the Kanemoto with both hands. My fall gave me an increased speed and the cut sliced his tattooed arm clean off. He let out a yell. When I last saw him, he was desperately trying to hold on to the Wind with his remaining hand.

I approached number two, a young man with a barbed spear, which he bravely threw at me. He grinned as he saw it hit my chest, but stopped when the spear glanced away. As I passed his legs, Kanemoto flashed, and I left him screaming as he fell.

Number three hung on to the Wind with both hands, and was

in a state of shock after seeing the two legs of number two, then number two himself, fall past him. I allowed him to be, as he looked innocent enough. A teenager.

"You are in bad company," I shouted as I dropped past him.

Number four turned out to be a girl of my age, sobbing as she clung with one hand at the wind and pointing a dagger at me with the other. I slowed down my fall, grabbed the wind and stood beside her.

"Why are you into this?" I asked.

She stabbed me in the chest but then, realising that I was invulnerable, threw away the dagger and sobbed, clinging on to my body.

"Is that your brother up there?" I asked.

She nodded. I felt then that these two were just a pair of misled youths, charmed by the idea of magic and power and enlisted into anything that would promise them a taste of both. I signalled to the youth above us who was anxiously looking down on his sister. "We go down!" I shouted. "*Anyah Baling Katimu!*" The Grey Wind slowed and left us on the banks of the Caspian Sea.

One of the most memorable sights the world has to offer is the breaking of dawn over the Caspian, where ribbons of scarlet red and orange are on the horizon ready to push up the dark-blue shutters of the night's sky. We stood on the sandy bank, taking in the unfolding beauty of the new day as the cold wind blew in over the waves and through the reeds and long-abandoned fishing boats behind us. The two young people huddled close and frightened, wondering what I would do to them. They were brother and sister alright—both shared the same features of a Mongolian and Caucasian mix. Both had oriental cheekbones, oriental eyes but auburn hair.

"*Sibir?*—Siberia?"

"*Dah Dah!*" they replied together. So they spoke Russian, but I didn't. Only a few words learnt from the Hollywood films. To be able to ride the Grey Wind, they must have had some training in Mysticism, so I pointed to a spot some three feet above our heads and they nodded in understanding. We would use our thoughts to converse, talk being unnecessary. By focusing on that spot above us, I first projected an image of the first man I met coming down, the one with that tattooed arm. They returned with an image of him in a smoked-filled den, chanting over a few sacred objects. The next image was of him taking them in hand to ride the Wind.

I then showed them an image of the second man with the barbed spear. They replied with a vision of him in blue jeans injecting himself in the arm, and shook their heads to express their disapproval. Next, I projected an image of themselves and they returned with a picture of a small village in the countryside, with rye and rape fields growing side by side—there was an avenue of silver birches, and probably their house on the right, with white walls and a blue door.

They then showed me a city, tramlines and buses with smoky exhausts, and of meeting the man with the tattoos and their being brought by him to a café. They showed me how ravenously they ate as they wolfed down the food and then the last scene being the smoke-filled den with those two men.

I decided what was best for them, so I showed them the image of their home, with that long avenue of trees and the fields of rape and rye.

"*Dah! Dah! Karasho!*" she shouted, clapping her hands.

I motioned them to stick close by as I waited for the sight of another Grey Wind. It finally came just as the sun was above the horizon, I caught it and they followed holding on for their dear lives. The wind moved northwards, just as we'd hoped. Before long, we found ourselves over the great expanse called Siberia. It was just after midday when the girl gripped me on the arm and pointed to a place below.

"Home? *Dom?*" I asked. She nodded excitedly, while shouting at her brother for his attention. I slowed down the wind and alighted on a deserted road. They stood there expecting me to make the next move. I just smiled and shook my head "No scoldings or lessons from me, so go!" I ordered.

But before we parted, I projected the horrifying images of the slaying of Mrs. Newas and the Indian Holy Man as a warning. Then, as a parting gift, I showed the young man a picture of himself in a business suit in front of a new car. He was pleased to no end. And for the young girl, a vision of herself coming out of a church dressed in a wedding gown. She gave me a hug and ran off down their country road towards home.

That task completed, I walked for a bit on the dirt road and wondered about my own folks back home. This set of parents, my grandmother, my friends and Fat Aunt. Then my thoughts took me to Pak Samad, Aweh and to Sri.

Sri—would she be there for me? And then, what about my Kumiko in Japan?

Chapter Thirty Three

"Go to Britain," Pak Samad had ordered. But where to in Britain?

Then I remembered Aweh's parting words, to let the "dark lights guide you."

My anger at the loss of Kohima, the loss of my men and my last life, the loss of the War and the reduction of our Emperor to a mere mortal by the Western Allies gave me an added will to hurry on.

I picked on the fastest Wind that I could see going that way and we swept over the great expanse that is Europe. I ignored all the green lights and the dark red ones shooting up to the sky. There would be others to do battle with them; my task was to take on my former teki or enemy, the British.

It didn't take me long to cross the channel, Britain lay below me; here and there I could see the green rays of light seeking the sky and a few dark red ones doing the same.

No, those were not worthy of battle. I wanted the coming fight to be the biggest battle of my life, and so I resolved to seek the source of the darkest light.

As I travelled up the island of Britain, I was pleased to see the green beams outnumber the dark ones.

I supposed there were more "White witches" than the Black ones as I flew northwards.

Just at the Scottish border on their Eastern coast, a dark beam suddenly shot upwards to meet me. I managed to duck as it passed on its way to the Heavens, as though to announce its presence to those opposed to its Dark power.

That was the strongest Dark Beam of Mystic light I had ever seen on this land.

"Anyah Baling Katimu!" and I came down on the Caledonian border, Northumberland, the land wet, dark and cold. I went into Hari Kong almost immediately.

Pak Samad and Sri were there to meet me. Sri came forward and gave me a hug and that 'bottle of Codeine' feeling again as the warmth of her being re-entered my soul. She looked as attractive as ever dressed in the finery of a lady-in-waiting.

Meanwhile Pak Samad, in his whites and with those different coloured shoes, laughed and shook his pointed umbrella towards the ground.

"Want some fruits?" he asked.

Sri and I laughed politely at his idea of humour at this grave juncture. I was almost sick thinking of what was to come. "No fruits, Pak, battle first!"

"Who are these Black Magicians that I am about to face?" I asked.

"Si Jan, they are a great source of Evil on this land and beyond," Pak Samad replied.

"They are the successors of the Templar Knights in Palestine who had sworn to protect the pilgrims from the Moors during the Crusades. They returned to Europe with their loot from the Holy Land and, when they were hounded out of France, they brought their treasures here, to Britain. By then, the oaths they took to do only Good had evaporated in exchange for Power over all Men and revenge on those who opposed them. When their old leaders had died out, they summoned the Dark Forces to help them achieve that aim. As you know, it is easier to deal with the Devil than to find God; just as it is easier to roll down a hill, than to climb up it.

With their new-found powers, they started to do mischief of all kinds, from causing suffering to their own countrymen and to the start of conquests of other nations spreading their cruelty further afield. All the time, they were in the service of the Dark Forces in exchange for untold wealth and position.

"Right now, they are in that ruined church beyond those Roman ruins," Pak Samad said and pointing with his umbrella. "That is where they hid their greatest treasure, the Ark, which they stole from Palestine during the Crusades."

"Wow! Ark of the Covenant?" I asked. As schoolboys, we had watched the film 'The Ten Commandments', with Charles Heston as Moses parting the waves of the Red Sea, and the Jews with their religious artifacts on the way to their 'Promised Land'.

Now to be told by this five- or six-hundred year old warrior, that it was in fact true and not just a Hollywood creation. I could only look at him with disbelief.

Sri gave my arm a squeeze and nodded. "It's true, believe our Pak Samad".

"Well, what am I supposed to do? Whom do you want me to get rid of?" I asked.

"Destroy any who oppose you, as they will reveal their hostility when you show yourself, then seize the Ark, pry open its cover and release the Light back to where it came from".

"Si Jan, do that for us, as we can't do it ourselves."

"Why can't you?"

"We could before and very easily too, but, at our stage, we

cannot kill any more humans. Only you and Aweh can," came his answer.

"Hah! So you want me to do the dirty work? "I thought to myself.

"Yes," Pak Samad replied, reading my thoughts.

"You were chosen the day you were born, our half-killer and half-Mystic. What you turn out to be, in the years to come, depends on how you lead your life. Left alone, you have the talent to become either a Black Magician with the most sinister intentions, or a White one that will one day reach the Light."

"Here", he said, handing me the bangle of Black Coral, "you left this behind."

Sri brought out the keris that Pak Samad had given me at our wedding. "I don't need two of you now," she smiled.

Fixing my thoughts, I transformed myself into a Malay warrior, with my own keris, Kyai Aweng, made by Aweh, tucked into the front of my sarong and the Laksamana's keris tucked in the back.

We moved in Hari Kong towards the ruined church. We could hear the chanting of prayers as we entered the ruins; they sounded Latin and also in Hebrew and Arabic, which was most unusual.

Arranged in two rows and facing each other were men dressed

in white cassocks, with a design of an upside-down Cross in red, emblazoned on the front and back. They all wore hoods of black except the one at the altar, who wore one of red. Pak Samad pointed to him. "That's the leader, kill him first and all the others who come towards you."

"Their version of the Ark is that small affair, that box placed between the two rows of men," he added.

Their so-called 'Ark of the Covenant' looked like any old tin chest from a junk shop. There were no wings of gold, no gilded calf, or whatever Hollywood had suggested. However, I could see the straps of thick leather and buckles of gold binding this box, so I knew it must be something of importance to these hooded men.

The leader of the group in his white robe and the red hood intoned more prayers or chants as we watched.

Pak Samad tapped me on the shoulder. "Get ready!"

My mind worked feverishly to form a plan of attack, and to decide when was the right time to do so. There was about a hundred of them in that church; how many of them had weapons concealed under their robes? And what about this Black Lord that they were summoning?

A Dark Shadow started forming. First, the naked feet became visible, then the legs, well-proportioned, then the lower hairy body, the muscular chest, the arms, and finally the head.

"It's Tristan Barnaby, the leading politician, a Cabinet Minister!" I yelled. Pak Samad nodded. "These days, the Dark Forces are everywhere, the world has changed so much so that it is hard to know who is human and who is not. Their aim now is to turn this world into Night, leaving out the Light. For life to exist, there must be a proper balance between Light and the Darkness. Without the balance, too much of either, whether it is too much of day or night, this world would be destroyed."

I gripped Kyai Aweng's hilt hard. I had formulated a plan and I hoped that my trusty keris would do as ordered.

Pak Samad made a slit in Hari Kong the moment the politician had fully materialised. "Si Jan! Go!" he ordered.

I dashed out. "Kyai Aweng! Change into a kukri Nepali!" I shouted. The keris transformed itself into the heavier kukri blade. I made a beeline for the Ark and hacked at the old leather straps and then at the lid of the Ark. Though covered by tin or brass of some kind, it shattered quite easily and the cedar or acacia beneath, dried for a few hundred years, almost exploded when the kukri struck.

I could only see half of a small stone tablet inside, and not two stone tablets as the Bible said. There was a stunned silence from all sides, followed by a rumbling inside the Ark.

Like a switch being thrown, a thick beam of green light shot up towards the night sky. The politician cowed on the ground. "*Kyai Aweng! Pedang Jepun!*"

Once again, the keris transformed itself into my Kanemoto and it swung into action. I beheaded the politician and rushed to meet the one with the red hood, but he turned out to be faster than I; covering his face with his cloak, he turned aside and was gone in an instant.

I then turned to meet the crowd who charged at me with swords held high. Due to the narrowness of the aisle, they could only come at me four abreast. I could see that there were sixteen of them, arranged in lines of four, one line behind the other.

I knelt on one knee and waited for the first line to reach me. The four screaming men, their eyes glaring, came at me with their Scottish basket-hilted swords held high.

What a poor move, and such an untutored lot. In battle, one is best advised to keep a cool head, if it is to stay firmly attached to one's neck.

In the half kneeling position, my sword slashed upwards and across their chests, at a line below their armpits. As the Kanemoto blade travelled, their swords dropped to the ground. Two of the men managed a groan before choking on their own blood. The other two just crumpled, without much ceremony.

I smiled as the next four came forward, swords raised, ready to cut me down. I could sense that Pak Samad and Sri would be watching, so I decided to give them a show of what a good Japanese swordsman can do with a decent blade.

I laughed as I stabbed the middle two in their throats in quick succession, then, turning my blade edge upwards, I went for the jugular of the one on my right; having done so, my blade made a twist, then a horizontal slash at the remaining man on my left. He managed to swing his sword upwards to meet my attack, but, speed being the essence of this art, my sword came down to meet his wrist before flying upwards to behead him.

The rest of the congregation turned and fled leaving the few trapped between the aisle, brave enough to confront me.

The floor now slippery with blood, I re-assumed the half kneeling position as the next four came at me. One threw his sword at me, hitting me in the chest but it bounced away. "I have Spirit of Cane, Sir!" I called out in English, "Spirit of Cane!" As I rose up from my kneeling position, this time I charged at them for a change. Their bodies fell sideways between the pews; one jerked his legs like a beheaded chicken before becoming still.

The next four retreated, carrying their old swords with them. I was not told to take prisoners, so I launched into a frenzied killing spree. I slashed at the backs of the middle two and as they went down, I was able to reach the two on the sides. One screamed like a woman as he turned to face me, while the other was more interested in trying to get away by running into a pew.

"No one escapes!" I said to myself as I ran after him. My sword managed to cut at the base of his neck. I could feel the grating of steel on bone.

"That should be good enough," I said to the screaming man behind me as I turned towards him.

"Please God, have mercy! Mercy!" he pleaded, throwing down his sword.

"A merciful God is an unjust God!" If everyone could be forgiven, what was the use of a Hell?

"May God take me the way I now take you!" I suppose those were the last words he took with him to his corner of heaven.

It had taken me only a few minutes to finish my work. There were two men left, probably in their eighties, kneeling on the floor, begging forgiveness. I gave them none. "You should have changed, repented, when you were young!"

Despite so much blood and death around me, or maybe because of it, I felt a sense of exhilaration. Something had come back to me from some bloodthirsty past—maybe from an earlier lifetime, perhaps the late Muromachi period of old Japan? Or on the plains of Sekigahara? I made a mental note to ask Pak

Samad. Was I in Sekigahara too? The name kept coming into my mind. Sekigahara! Was it he who told me that I have had a whole lot of lives before? Or was it Fat Aunt? I was no longer sure.

Pak Samad appeared behind me and nodded, as though approving of my work.

"I am sorry I failed to kill their leader—he was too fast for me. I made a mistake. I should have gone for him before beheading that politician, and I am sorry to have let so many go."

"No, you have done enough for today. This is just the start of your battles; there will be more. One can't meet with success every single time, life would get too boring. After all, the enemies you slaughtered there were just packets of energy, now dissipated back to our Universe. Hopefully they will be reformed and return as better beings.

"It is well that we sent the huge Power of Good back, so the Balance between Good and Evil can now be easier to restore."

"So, Pak Samad, where do you want me to go from here?"

"You can go home to your parents in Singapore."

"What about Sri?"

"Sri is an *Orang Bunyiaan*—she will live forever. Maybe you will too as you are almost one of us now. You can come and see Sri whenever. But I would advise that the two of you be together only under our skies—we can't trust Mankind anymore."

"Come to us, Si Jan whenever you want to, travel by the Wind or if necessary through Hari Kong. We will stretch Time for as long as we want for ourselves, and when you return home, it would only be a few hours or a day," Sri whispered.

"And what about my own sword that I used in World War Two? You promised!"

"Yes, Si Jan, we did. It is with a Professor Prendergast who lives in Santry, Dublin in Ireland. He will hold on to it for you until you get there. The time is not ripe. You will have many more adventures. Such is your life. To be what you will ultimately become, you need to undergo more heartbreaks and sorrow, more trials." Then, he added, almost as an afterthought and giving me a wink, "the more the temper, the better the steel, as they would say in Japan!"

Big deal! I thought to myself. "But, Laksamana, I have yet to discover who I was before."

"Remember what I told you, not so long ago, Si Jan? It is not important for a man to know what he was before. It is more important to know what he is now, and what he will be in the future."

"What about my old name?"

"You mean Captain Ichiro Sato of the 138 Regiment in

Burma?" he replied, laughing for the world to hear.

Sri tried to pacify me. "Come Si Jan, let's all just ride the Wind."

Chapter Thirty Four

We rode in silence for a while as the Wind carried us across the Continent. Sri hugged me with her free hand and snuggled closer, burying her face in my neck and planting little kisses whenever she saw Pak Samad looking the other way.

Pak Samad, now changed back to the ancient warrior with his eyes fixed on the brightening sky of a new dawn, ignored us. A little later, he looked down at me, still sulking, and smiled.

"Si Jan, or Captain Ichiro Sato, what good is it to know what you were in your past life? Now that you know, what can you do about it? That is why I said it is better to know what you are now and what you will become in the future. You are now just another nineteen year old, with battle experience in this life and in your past life, but with nothing else achieved to live in this world of Man."

Pak Samad paused, looked at me, smiled, then looked away

for a moment before continuing.

"You will have to work hard to live on. Your life as a Mystic will not be a smooth one; you decided your own fate when you became a student of your Fat Aunt. Use the experience you have gained so far in this life, in your previous ones, and the magic we have taught you; these things should help in the years to come. You will have to work to make a living like any man, though the battles that you will have to fight will be different."

And as though reading my thoughts, he added, "Yes, you were also in Sekigahara but stupidly fought on the wrong side in sixteenth century Japan. It was a bloody war and it turned you into a wandering master-less samurai, a Ronin. That was all in the past, which explains why you are so deadly with a sword. You have just killed twenty men all on your own. It had to be done, sad to say, as the world will be facing a crisis soon."

"Just know and remember that it is a thankless job. Mankind is always grateful for the wrong things or to the wrong people. You will be just another star in the sky; its possible that no one will know you ever existed."

"I know, Pak Samad," I said. "Who wants to be famous? I'll just do my job and try to make this world a happier place."

"We have armed you with the magic of Invulnerability and the art of Invisibility so that you can carry out our tasks without harm to yourself. We have only shown you the way, soon you will be on your own and must acquire the ability to decide, to judge and act accordingly."

Once again, Pak Samad threw back his head and laughed, his long hair trailing in the wind. Now looking more like what he was in our nation's history, as Hang Tuah our national hero, the Laksamana, or Admiral of the Malaccan Sultanate. No more of those black and white shoes and that magical umbrella.

Dark clouds of the coming monsoon were forming ahead as we moved on. Soon the lands would be drenched and only the water buffaloes would be happy.

"We will get off here now, Si Jan," Pak Samad said. "Will you go on home?"

Steeling myself against the hurt of another parting, I answered in the affirmative.

"I will, Pak Samad. Thank you for everything. I will never forget you."

"How can you?" He threw his head back and laughed again.

Sri gripped my hand and looked at me with those pleading eyes. "Si Jan, just know that I will wait, and take care."

I gave her the keris that I had got from Pak Samad.

"Let this keris be me, Sri," I whispered, "and look after him."

She nodded, clutching the weapon closer to her chest.

"*Anyang Baling Katimu!*" The Grey Wind slowed, allowing them to slide down to the ground. They stood there waving, and watched me as I moved on.

Sleepy Singapore lay just ahead, half of that tropical island then still covered by jungle. I came down unnoticed on a vegetable patch in Mong Hiang's garden.

I strolled to where the Japanese trenches were, had a last look at the past, and walked home.

"*Natsu gusa ya, tsuwamono domo no, yume no ato* —Fields of summer grasses are all that remain … of a Warrior's dream." —Basho, 17th century Japan.

The End

Background Information

Keris: The keris is quintessentially a weapon peculiar to the peoples of Indonesia, Malaysia, Brunei and the Southern Thailand.

Often viewed as a talisman more than a weapon, many kerises are believed to contain a Spirit or Guardian that will protect its owner. It may warn of imminent danger by rattling in its sheath or by other omens, like dreams, but it may also cause the owner harm if not treated with due respect.

Until the beginning of the last century, no man was considered dressed if seen without a keris on his person. These days, they are still worn on ceremonial occasions.

A keris blade may be sinuous, with waves like a moving snake or straight. The patterns on the blade suggest the type of power that the keris may possess.

A man's keris may be used to represent him if he is unable to attend in person.

Kukri: A weapon of the Nepalese and carried by their famous soldiers, the Gurkhas.

Kanemoto: Name of a famous swordsmith in old Japan. His blades are known for their extreme sharpness and strength.

Mandau: A head hunter's sword from Borneo, usually with bunches of a victim's hair on the scabbard.